Leannán Sidhe

Leannán Sidhe

THE IRISH MUSE & OTHER STORIES

Brian O'Sullivan

STEELE ROBERTS
AOTEAROA NEW ZEALAND

for Saoirse and Takaterangi

© Brian O'Sullivan 2007

National Library of New Zealand
Cataloguing-in-Publication Data
O'Sullivan, Brian, 1965-
Leannán Sidhe : the Irish muse
and other stories / Brian O'Sullivan.
ISBN 978-1-877448-07-2
I. Title.
NZ823.3—dc 22

STEELE ROBERTS PUBLISHERS
BOX 9321 WELLINGTON, AOTEAROA NEW ZEALAND
info@steeleroberts.co.nz • www.steeleroberts.co.nz

Contents

Acknowledgements	6
Leannán Sidhe	7
Drowning in daylight	22
Ag suansiúl as Béarla — Sleepwalking in English	25
After the beep	45
The Ringmaster's daughter	53
Sex with Sarah	72
The morning after	87
Fridge	94
Foreign correspondent	97
Suddenly, a valley	115
Slither	121
Cinema	131
Morris dancing	135

Acknowledgements

'Fridge' — *Takahe* 43 (2001)
'Movie' — *JAAM* 16 (2001) and *Takahe* 44 (2002)
'Drowning in Daylight' — *Electric Acorn* (2003)
'Foreign Correspondent' — *Carve* Magazine (2003)

The triskele or triple spiral is a Celtic and pre-Celtic symbol found on a number of Megalithic and Neolithic sites in Ireland. The most famous of these is on the entrance stone to the passage tomb at Brú na Bóinne (Newgrange).

Leannán Sidhe

I watch her cycle in from Gaineamh Dubh, her face tired and damp from the evening rain. Long copper curls twist in the wind like wire behind a face of stone. Her eyes fixed firmly on her destination. Icicles hang from her handlebars.

The seat outside Goleen post office is a secure perch to watch the girl go by — a blur of whirling spokes and curls against the sunset. Four weeks earlier, back in New Zealand, I'd observed a different sunset in the sea off Kapiti but even then there'd been a tenuous connection with the village of Goleen. I was already anticipating the bright clutter of houses nestled in the grey Galway coast, the sensation of ice against my skin and black rocks encrusted with yellow lichen.

The following afternoon I come across the girl again, behind the counter of Coughlan's pub. The bar is quiet at the height of the low season, empty apart from a German couple arguing softly in the corner.

I study her as she scoops Irish stew from a pot into a pair of yellow bowls and realise that she's younger than I'd imagined, no older than twenty-three or twenty-four. In the dim light behind the counter her face looks less severe, unburdened by the resolute expression she wears when pedalling against the wind.

Sensing my presence, she looks up from the pot, eyes still warm from the heat of it. They flicker over me briefly then fall to the silver fern on the backpack slung over my shoulder.

"You're a New Zealander." Her voice is surprisingly husky; a richly lacquered rawness.

"Yes. How did you know?"

"Ah, me Da spent some time over there once. He had a flag with a fern like that on it."

"Uh-huh."

I place my glass on the counter, my gaze sliding down the length of polished teak to an old violin and bow lying cushioned on a stack of dated newspapers. The girl follows my gaze.

"It's the house fiddle. Coughlan leaves it out for any musician who wants to borrow it for the sessions." She considers me appraisingly. "It's still in pretty good nick."

"May I?"

She shrugs.

"Knock yourself out."

I pick up the instrument, softly pluck each string to test the sound of it then slip it beneath my chin. Closing my eyes, I raise the bow and release a long chord into the silence of the room.

I play the basis of a melody that's been in my head for several weeks — scraps of an elusive tune I've been trying to develop for a television commercial — something suitably Celtic to accompany the latest in European sports car as it thunders through some iconic Irish valley.

Starting from the basic motif, I improvise on the rhythm around it, visualising the music as it careens through the valley, bouncing off rock cliffs and spiralling into the ether on a stream of tumultuous air currents. Then I reach that sequence of notes where it all goes wrong. The music spins in one direction, the soul of the tune in another, its beauty unravelling in a spiral of sound. The chords slide off the fiddle to tumble gracelessly into the room like dead space.

Cursing, I lower the instrument and replace it on the counter, glaring at it furiously until I remember where I am. Looking up, I find the girl watching me.

"That was beautiful! Why did you stop?"

Her question momentarily throws me.

"Because that's all there is."

She looks at me blankly but failure has left me drained and withdrawn. Shaking my head, I mumble goodnight and turn to leave the pub.

Her eyes are heavy on my shoulders as I step into the twilight.

Daylight blows in on the tail of a westerly gale, a brutal flurry that thrashes the coastline and threatens to toss startled sheep through the valleys like tumbleweed.

I remain confined to my B&B, trapped between the pelting rain and threads of the commercial music rattling at the back of my mind. I spend several frustrating hours twisting various arrangements over and over again in my head, never quite able to capture the essence of the tune.

Thwarted, I brave the deluge that evening to wander down to Coughlan's and dilute my frustration in a mellow whiskey. At six o'clock the girl comes in to take a shift, serving the regulars with an easy grace as she listens to their grumbles or laughs at their jokes. She has an agreeably distinctive laugh — a melodious sequence of descending notes that drops sharply to be obliterated by a mercilessly deep chuckle.

At eight o'clock she stops pulling pints, extracts a silver flute from a box behind the counter and joins the musicians crowding out the snug. The flute gleams in the yellow firelight as the first lonely chord resonates in the confines of the snug then seeps into the hubbub of the public lounge. Conversations lapse as the mournful notes drift through the crowd, leaving a startled desolation behind like the wake of a passing phantom.

There's a stunned silence when the tune finally draws to a close. The patrons blink and shake their heads until the musicians commence a thigh-slapping jig that rattles everybody from their stupor, then once again it's a typical Friday night in a rural Irish lounge bar.

The musicians play without stop for the next ten minutes and as the music continues, spinning seamlessly from one tune to the next it becomes apparent that they're engaged in some competition of endurance. I stare at the faces of the musicians, blank with concentration as the pace continues to escalate and the air is repeated and amplified in volume. Surprisingly, it's the younger players who display the first signs of fatigue, reluctantly dropping out as the older musicians hang in with a tenacity borne of a lifetime's playing.

After twenty minutes only two of the musicians remain — the girl with her flute and an elderly banjo player — playing an energetic polka at an increasingly frenzied tempo. Suddenly, the banjo player, red-faced and panting, allows his banjo to fall by his side. Although she sees him drop out, the girl plays on for another minute, building up momentum on the cusp of the tune before releasing her soul in the ecstatic rip of the final bars.

There's a thunderous round of applause as the girl lowers her instrument and her eyes gleam as her back is pounded. When the excitement settles, however, she seems relieved to slip away, sidling over to my dark little corner to sip her drink and savour her achievement in silence. After a moment or two, she notices me, stiffening slightly as recognition hits her.

"Hallo," I say.

"Hallo. You're back then?"

"I am."

"Are you playing with us?"

"Too much like hard work." I swallow a mouthful of warm whiskey. "That was impressive."

"No." Her response is dismissive. "That was just practice."

"I was talking about your first tune."

She regards me curiously and I can tell that she's trying to make me out, get some sense of the stranger behind the accent.

"I was thinking …"

"Yeah."

"That tune you played last night …"

"What about it?"

"I was just curious. It seemed to be building up to something beautiful but then you stopped and left it hanging there like …"

I wait for her to continue but she simply shakes her head and places her glass on the table.

Although reluctant to discuss it I'm impressed that she'd sensed it — that sliver of beauty concealed in the muddle of notes I'd been playing.

"It's something I've been working on. I haven't quite pulled it together just yet."

One eyebrow arches curiously.

"You're a composer?"

"Yes."

"Would I know any of your work?"

"Unlikely. I've put out five CDs of my own compositions over the years but they haven't sold much outside Australasia. Most of my stuff is incidental music for advertisements in New Zealand and Australia."

The girl swirls her glass. The ice rattles against the sides. "I don't think I could write music. I mean, I can interpret a tune creatively enough — play around with it or adjust its various elements to make it sound the way I think it should — but it always remains within the limits of the original composition. That's traditional music for you, though." She dips a finger in her drink and stirs the ice cubes. "Creating something completely original, now that's a different ballgame! I mean, how do you create something out of nothing?"

I breathe deeply and put my glass aside.

"Creating something's the easy part. The difficult part is finding the inspiration, the flicker of sensation that ignites the process."

"Why's that so hard?"

"Probably because it's so simple. Inspiration's an instinctive process without rules. Anything can act as a stimulus — a memory, a snatch of an old song, an evocative scent — anything that provokes a reaction to fit the space you're trying to fill at the time."

"You make it sound complex."

I laugh at that.

"That's the problem with simple things. When you restrict them with definition they start to become incredibly complex. It's probably best to just accept it. Creativity without inspiration is like sex without affection — you're simply going through the motions."

Her lips curve in an enigmatic smile.

"Sounds like you need a Leannán Sidhe."

"A what?"

"A Leannán Sidhe." She considers me again with that same cryptic grin. "In Irish folklore, the Leannán Sidhe's a kind of fairy muse that takes an artist for a lover. In return for her lover's affection she bestows a gift on him; the ability to create a work of art of immense feeling."

She turns and for a second or two her profile is outlined against the lustre of the fire behind her. In that precise moment I experience an unexpectedly profound sense of connection between us; some deep, fundamental attraction that extends across the abyss of age and culture.

She turns her head and her green eyes smoulder in the glow of the fire.

"My name," she says, "is Moira."

We move closer to the musicians but she doesn't rejoin the session, remaining instead by the entrance of the snug to converse while unconsciously tapping out the rhythm of the tune with her foot. I find myself repeatedly distracted by the sound of her accent, the singsong brogue that hangs in the air like a half-heard fragment of distant music.

It's the whiskey, of course. The whiskey, the rawness of the traditional music and the heightened sensitivity brought on by heated proximity to a sensual young woman. I should know better but my skin still tingles when our knees touch.

Time to go, I think to myself.

I'm in the process of rising from my seat when she turns and looks at me with those full green eyes. The tangle of red curls burn like embers in the ashes of her grey jersey and I'm vaguely aware of the trad group slapping bodhrán sticks and making their fiddles scream. We kiss passionately over the 'Long Yellow Road'. The rest is an incoherent blur. There is smothering warmth in her bed, moist, tender sensation beneath her blankets. There is a day. There is a night. And then there is another day.

Daylight reveals the reality of Moira's 'apartment' — a single room in a boarding house at the tip of Gaineamh Dubh pier. There are two windows inscribed with Jack Frost's signature swirls, a raggedy bed with a red duvet and a tall teak wardrobe that looks like a vertical coffin. Her flute and a battered guitar rest on the floor between the bed and a table piled high with books. An ancient sink in the corner has one tap missing. The hot one.

My head throbs as I shift beneath the sheets. There's a rustle of movement and a supple form folds about me.

"Hi, stranger."

Her voice sounds even throatier, hoarse from too much talking and too much kissing.

"Good morning."

"Sleep well?"

"Like the dead. I'm getting too old for this."

"You're not that old, grand-dad."

"Actually today's another nail in the coffin. It's my birthday."

"Go 'way! What age?"

"Forty-five."

"Old enough to be me Da."

"Jesus!"

Laughing, she leans over to the bedside table. Pulling two cigarettes from a wrinkled cigarette packet, she lights them with a bronze-plated zippo and hands one to me.

"Happy birthday, old man."

She makes coffee in an antique *cafetiére*. Steam from the lip of the vessel is swallowed up by the cold bite in the air. Outside, the day looms ominously cloudy and the pier reverberates to the chug of a fishing boat coming home from the sea. She stands by the window, a tense white silhouette against the dark mountains and I regard her athletic flanks and tight stomach, the body taut with the suppressed vitality of a compressed spring.

"What do you think?" She gestures at the view outside.

"It's beautiful."

The reflection in the window grins cynically.

"Only a tourist would say that. The locals would call it 'god-forsaken'."

"You're not a local?" I ask cautiously.

She shakes her head. "Anyone without at least five generations lying in the graveyard isn't a local. My family have only been here for fifty years so I'm still considered a 'blow-in'. Going off to study in Cork for years didn't earn me any credibility either."

"What did you study?"
She shrugs. "Music — what else? I did four years but never finished the degree."
"That seems a bit of a waste."
She scratches a fingernail against the frost on the windowpane.
"It was an intense time. My mother died when I was a child but I lost my father just before my final exams last year. I don't have any other family and at the time I needed to dismantle, to drain down and let all the shit bleed out. Otherwise, I would've exploded."
"It's still a waste. Surely your father would have wanted you to finish."
"I suppose that's true. Da was always at me to get some formal qualification. He'd be mad if he knew I'd ended up working in Coughlan's." She shrugs. "I know my job is menial, I know I don't earn much money but fuck it, it's only temporary. I have my bike and my books.
"And my music," she adds. "Most of all I've got my music."
She withdraws into herself then and says nothing more for over a minute. I pick up one of the battered books lying on the table.
"What's with all the books?"
"Fairytales."
Her sudden smile surprises me. "My Da used to read them to me as a kid and I didn't have the heart to throw them away." She takes a volume and tenderly rubs the cover. "I've always had a soft spot for fairytales. You know, fearless heroes, great passions and happy endings."
"Haven't we all," I say.

That afternoon we borrow a spare bike to cycle back the coast road over Sliabhmish hill. It's all I can do to keep up with her as she powers up the steep country lanes like a fury high on aviation fuel.
Down by the seashore, uneven squares of grass bordered by grey stone walls are blanketed in early morning frost. A mantle of snow on the mountain peaks rolls down to lap at the hard rock below the scree. The view is striking, the sheer volume of gnarled black rock both bleak and hauntingly beautiful all at once. I pull over to the side of the road.

"Christ, that's a view!"

Moira pulls up alongside to gaze at the snow-capped mountains then shrugs, immune to the beauty from years of residency. "Sugar powder," she says. "It softens the raw bite of the hills."

I realise then that's one of the things I like about Moira. She's a plain-speaker, a black coffee woman who requires no sweetener.

"You're quiet."

"Sorry. A few things on my mind."

"Are you composing?"

"What?"

"Are you thinking through that tune in your head? Sometimes I'll do that when I'm trying to work out some new variation."

"No. To be honest I'm shooting musical blanks."

"What?"

I lean against the handlebars and look at the view.

"Writer's block, Moira. I've had it for two years now. On a professional level, I've basically been living off variants of old works I did years ago. Last month I was obliged to take on a commission for a car commercial. Unfortunate really as everything I write now is so insubstantial it simply slides off the pages."

She glances at me cautiously.

"I'm not sure I can relate to that but it sounds … bad."

"It's a bit like losing a limb, or something very dear to you."

"I guess I can relate to that."

"Yes," I say. "I guess you probably can."

Tim Malone, the village postman passes by the apartment later that evening. Tim, known locally as 'Timbuctoot' due to an overwhelming pair of incisors, hands me a fax from Dublin addressed to 'The New Zealander'.

"It's marked *urgent*," he says eagerly. "Seeing as how you're the only New Zealander in the village I thought I'd bring it right here."

I don't ask him how he knew where to find me. This is, after all, a small village.

He places the single page on the table. It says: *Have a good trip home on Sunday!* The words are underlined by Hannah's characteristically flamboyant signature, scrawled like a stain across the clean white paper.

Moira and Timbuctoot look at me expectantly.

I fold the paper away and put it in my pocket.

"So who's Hannah?" asks Moira.

"An old friend from home. We played in a band together back in Wellington years ago. She's based in Dublin now."

They both stand there waiting for me to say something else but when nothing is forthcoming Moira turns to Tim. "Thanks, Timbuctoot. You can go now."

"What?"

She glares meaningfully at him for several seconds.

"Ah," says Timbuctoot, finally recognising his cue. "Ahem. Okay. I'd best be going. God bless now!"

Once we're alone, Moira sits on the bed and stirs a hot toddy in silent contemplation. Granules of sugar flicker like spinning diamonds in the amber liquid.

"Listen," she says at last, "you're not one of those sad married fuckers doing the mid-life crisis bit, are you?"

I sit on the bed beside her.

"I'm not the marrying kind, Moira. I've only ever considered it once and that was a shambles."

She regards me dubiously.

"What happened?"

"The age-old story. I met a girl. We fell in love and lived together for eighteen months. One day, out of the blue, she tells me that she wants to have children."

I stare quietly at the evening shadows swelling up around the windowpane.

"Unfortunately I didn't, so we split up. She went overseas. Two years ago I tried to look her up but found out she'd married an Irishman, separated, then died of a drug overdose up in Dublin."

"Jesus!"

"Yeah. That's what I thought."

We lie silently in the darkness for several minutes before Moira speaks again.

"Regrets?"

"Of course. There was a choice and I made the wrong decision. Now I have to live with that."

"I'm not looking for anything."

"What?"

"I'm not looking for anything. Promises or commitments. I understand you're going back to New Zealand." She coughs. "I can tell you're not completely comfortable with … me."

"I'm sorry. I guess I'm just aware of the differences between us."

"Like the age thing?"

"Yeah," I admit. "Like the age thing."

She's silent again for several seconds.

"Have you ever wondered why I don't have a boyfriend my own age, why none of the local boys make a pass at me?"

"It's crossed my mind," I admit.

"It's because they're scared of me. They find me too … intense. It intimidates them." She pauses. "You weren't intimidated."

She wraps an arm around me and eases closer.

That night in her sleep, she calls out for her father.

The village of Goleen is a kaleidoscopic huddle of brightly painted houses embedded in a landscape of grey rock. The harshness of this landscape is one of the reasons for the village's thriving music scene, its vitality an unconsciously animated reaction to the sombre surroundings.

Most of the village inhabitants are musically talented to some degree. Timbuctoot, for example, is an accomplished fiddler. Big Sally Reilly, from Reilly's Grocers has the body of a giant but the sweet singing voice of a child. Séamus the Fisherman, a blaspheming soul with a prosthetic hand, plays the guitar better than most musicians without such a disability. In Coughlan's, I've watched him calmly unlock a plastic hand from his wrist, snap a plectrum into place at the end of the stump, and strum while his other hand dances like a manic spider from chord to chord down the neck of his guitar.

Something about Moira, however, sets her apart from the other musicians in the village. Her music is raw and has an eerie undercurrent that's unsettling and profoundly moving in equal measure. It is also strangely erratic. Sometimes in the middle of a measured ballad she'll suddenly spin off on some otherworldly solo, eyes dilated in a frenzied paroxysm as she sends wild notes whirling off from the central air. You can sense the locals draw away from her, superstitiously misinterpreting such unaccustomed stylistic eccentricity as manifestations of some undiagnosed psychosis or dormant supernatural possession. It is only at such times that I fully appreciate the intimidating effect Moira has on the locals. They cannot see that she's still grieving, that she has learned to channel her pain through her instrument in bursts that leave her exhausted and empty but ultimately relieved.

On Friday night in Coughlan's snug, Sally Reilly informs the startled musicians that she's had enough of small town life and intends to leave for Dublin. On Saturday afternoon they gather at the bus stop to bid her farewell.

For once, the sun succeeds in piercing the froth of clouds and winter sunlight spills liquid gold onto the surrounding countryside. Someone has brought a guitar for Sally to sing one song before she goes. Someone else has brought a banjo and a tinwhistle. Moira has her flute and Sally just can't leave without one last song.

She sings 'Mo Ghile Mear' and follows that with 'Biddy Mulligan'. By the time she's finished the bus has arrived and the driver says are you getting on the bus or what? And she says one last tune, just one last tune.

'Willie MacBride'. Then 'Three Drunken Maidens'. And the driver says fuck this, I'm out of here. Everyone cheers and Sally's crying and says "Shit, I suppose I'd better stay after all!"

Someone strikes up a giddy reel and Sally's up there dancing in the middle of the street with Timbuctoot, sweeping her skirts up like a flamenco dancer.

The joyous whine of the fiddle supports Big Sally's voice. Moira's laughter is an almost perfect counterpoint to the chorus spinning off up into the mountain to echo around the fairy forts. I listen to that delicious peal of laughter; the one, two, three, four descending notes, the short sharp drop to a throaty chortle and for one moment everything just fits into place; the music, the hills, the valley, and Moira, all culminating in an experience so powerfully emotive it threatens to saturate my soul.

While the others withdraw the impromptu *céilí* to Coughlan's I hurry to Moira's flat, driven by a fragment of music so pure it sizzles in my head. Sitting at the table, I close my eyes, picture Moira's face and recall that laughter, drawing out its music and recapturing it in written form.

Within an hour, the elusive motif I've been forcing down a mountain path with a mundane motor vehicle is finally released as the emotional lament of a fairy queen keening to her lover from the human world. I look at the fluctuating series of aggregate notes written out on the paper before me and wonder how anything so beautiful and so simple could have eluded me for so long. When I close my eyes it lingers at the back of my head like the familiar voice of a long lost friend who's finally found his way home.

The musicians are playing hard when I get to Coughlan's. Taking a place at the crowded bar, I've time for a single drink before Moira sidles up bedside me.

"I need to show you something," she says in a voice that's slightly slurred. "Let's get the bikes!"

Amused, I follow her outside where we retrieve the bicycles and commence the ascent up the hills outside of town. Twenty-five gruelling minutes later we achieve the Sliabhmish heights and pull off the road. As we look down at the coast behind us, a full moon slides out from behind a huddle of cloud and the landscape is bathed in molten silver. Moonlight reflects on the harbour water and in the monochromatic light the exposed ridges and rock face are rendered as coarse as a lunar landscape.

"Now that's a view!" says Moira.

We stand there in silence for several minutes, inhaling the frigid beauty. In the end it's that same frosty edge that prompts us to return. My jaws ache from the ice on the breeze as we freewheel back to the village, hurtling like lunatics down the dark hillside, through valleys of craggy black rock. Our bicycle lamps shimmer on the bends and dip in the potholes, flickering through the darkness like epileptic fireflies. I'm barely aware of the cold, consumed instead by the solid black rushing up to meet me and the pulse of adrenaline as I plunge forward, blind to anything more than three feet in front of me.

Back in Moira's apartment, I tear at her clothing with hands numbed from the cold. Under frozen bed sheets my skin ignites at the brush of her fingertips and in the heave and shudder beneath the blankets we find each other again. When we finally draw apart, Moira wraps herself in the sheet and regards at me bleakly.

"You're leaving tomorrow."

"I figured I'd take the 10:30 bus to Dublin. That should give me enough time to catch my flight." I scratch the beginnings of stubble on my chin. "We should have spoken about this before, I know, but … it never seems to be the right time."

"Hey," she shrugs. "No promises, no commitments."

"Moira, there's something else."

She observes me warily.

"My friend Hannah works for a Dublin recording company who're making a compilation album of upcoming talent in the traditional scene. You'll be getting an invitation from them in a few days to go up and try out for it."

I consider her quietly.

"It'd be a unique opportunity if you were ever to consider a professional career."

She gives me a sceptical look.

"Why would they be inviting me?"

"Because I asked them to. You have a unique talent with that flute and it'd be crazy not to harness it. If you work with Hannah at the very least you'll know she'll play straight with you."

She looks at me uncertainly and for a moment it looks as though she's going to cry.

"Moira, you've outgrown Goleen. If you don't go out and use it, that potential's just going to fester up inside. Don't make a bad choice or you'll always regret what could have been."

She stares furiously at her flute for over a minute.

"All right," she says at last. "I'll accept the invitation." She sighs and lies back so her head is resting against the wall. "What about you? What are you going to do?"

"I've got my own career to resurrect back in Wellington. Thanks to you, I might just be able to do that. Oh, that reminds me."

I reach over to pull three folded sheets of notation paper from my greatcoat pocket, and hand them to her. Unfolding them, her eyes flicker over the combination of notes, automatically translating them to music in her head.

"This … it's the tune you were playing that first day." She smiles ruefully. "You've called it 'Stone Wall Muse'!"

"It wouldn't feel right to take it away. Besides, from here on in I'm hoping there'll be plenty more where that came from. My details are on the back if you want to contact me." I pause carefully. "That would always be welcome."

She picks up a book of fairytales and slides the papers inside the cover.

"Hardly a happy ending, is it?"

"There's no such thing as a happy ending — just different circumstances. Otherwise what would be the point?"

Moira doesn't come down to say goodbye when I leave the following morning, but as I wait by the bus stop the sound of her flute is audible through the upper windows of the boarding house. The music hangs faintly in the morning air, and it's only as the bus pulls in that I realise she's playing 'Stone Wall Muse'.

And I smile to myself for she hasn't been able to stop herself.

And has already made a new variation.

Drowning in daylight

The night is a coal pit, the road to An Gaillimh a perforated streamer of yellow lamps that stretches to infinity. It takes approximately six seconds to travel between each lamp. I count one potato, two potato, three potato, four potato, five potato, six potato then the Mercedes explodes into the next bubble of shimmering yellow.

There's an abrupt metallic flash. A green road sign with white writing.

An Gaillimh
GALWAY

Then black again.

"Please don't stop."

I can feel Nessa's eyes on me in the next burst of yellow.

"I don't think I can face an empty apartment tonight. Not after that argument."

Silence.

"Where do you want to go?"

"I don't know."

Nessa must be in a susceptibly sympathetic mood, for she squeezes down on the accelerator as we approach the city turn-off. A surge of power flows through the battered vehicle and the off-ramp is left behind us.

I slip down further into my seat, into the greatcoat that's a size too large. Despite the tepid air wheezing from the heater, the car remains uncomfortably cold. Rainwater freezes into thin white blades on the windscreen wipers. Fragments of melting snow, refrozen, lie fastened to the bonnet like molten limpets.

Further up the road we encounter a lump of fog that's thick and grey and viscous as porridge. In the gleam of fog-lamps we slide through yellow tendrils of mist floating in the air around us like the ghosts of dead jellyfish.

We drive for almost an hour without speaking. Nessa twists the knobs of the radio and is finally rewarded with a burst of classical music. The signal is weak, however, and in seconds it has faded away, dissolved in a stream of static. Shortly after, we turn off for the coast.

Nessa slips the car out of gear and we freewheel down a narrow track to the beach. Gravel crunches beneath the tyres as we pull off the road. When the car has come to a halt, I undo the safety belt, open the door and walk away from the car. No more than a few metres down the beach. It's so dark it's almost impossible to see.

I find a rock that's large enough to sit on and settle down to stare out in the direction of the sea. Unable to see the waves, I listen to them instead, enjoying the frothy gush as they surge up the beach and rattle the stones together with a sound like crackling bones.

Up by the car I hear the creak of the driver's door. There's a rustle of clothing, the click of a lighter and Nessa's face is illuminated in a small yellow flame. It flickers out, replaced by a red cigarette tip that glows like an ember in the night.

I move away. Further into the darkness where light cannot touch me.

I start to release the ache then. On my knees, in the sand. In small, deep breaths. There is no pain worse than the ending of love, no sense of loneliness so acute. No sense of despair so all-consuming. The end of love slashes you with a serrated edge. It chops up emotions with liquid, wicked relish and uses them for salad dressing.

Nessa sits up on the bonnet of the car, smokes, and waits. Her outline is a dim silhouette against the first grey light of dawn. After a while she finishes her cigarette, glances down at the beach, then returns to sit inside the car.

It's at such times that I am glad of such a friend. Nessa understands that my pain is private, that I ease bad lovers out of my life in long, soft silences. That's the most beautiful thing about friends. You can share things with them you would never share with lovers.

Unlike me, Nessa hides her pain deep and out of sight. I've seen her contain it for months on end until one day it finally erupts and I have to restrain her as she screams and kicks and exorcises her love in drunken, vicious bursts. She physically expels it, churning the hurt out of her heart and onto the grey stones of the west coast.

In the end it doesn't really matter. We both share the same pain and that makes us equal.

Dawn is heaving in around the coast and somehow I know it's going to be a beautiful day, just when I need it most. A day of emerald seas and pure white waves, a day of gleaming sunshine and children's laughter.

Beneath skies of sheer blue silk we find strength to draw back from the brink of our fears. They drown with the coming of dawn, floundering on the beach like a fish deserted by the tide.

Back at the car I find Nessa asleep in the driver's seat, looking so peaceful that for several minutes I don't have the heart to disturb her. Instead I sit on the bonnet of her car and smoke. Later, perhaps, I'll touch her on the shoulder and whisper "Everything's all right. We can go home now."

Ag suansiúl as Béarla —
Sleepwalking in English

Insomnia haunted me like a lovesick phantom. Smudge-eyed and brain-fried, by the time I got to Lille my reactions were sluggish, my perceptions deadened from days of sleep deprivation.

I took the metro from the railway station — a cylinder of light that slid through the subterranean darkness like a glimmer of hope in desperate circumstances. At the suburb of Wazemmes I emerged to a place where tendrils of icy vapour floated through the streets and the chill air brushed everything with a frostbitten Midas gesture.

The boarding house in Rue Manuel was a converted three-storey house with crumbling walls and a weatherbeaten red door. When I pressed the doorbell it seemed an eternity until the door swung open and a slim female stood silhouetted against the light from the hallway. She turned to face me, half of her face obscured by shadow, the other half illuminated by the inside light, and appraised me with one critical brown eye.

"*Ouai?*"

"I'm Donnacha."

"Ah!" She sniffed noncommittally and cast a glance over my shoulder as though expecting someone else. "*Veuillez entrer,*" she said at last and I crossed the threshold, quitting the glacial blackness for the illusion of warmth from amber illumination.

We examined each other more closely in the hallway. She looked to be in her late twenties, boyishly slim with short, black hair. She was attractive in a grungy kind of way but radiated a haughty intensity that made her appear remote and unfriendly. Despite the temperature she was barefoot and dressed in nothing more than a thin jersey and jeans.

She turned brusquely and indicated I should follow. We climbed the wide wooden stairs to the second floor, then went down a narrow corridor to a room with an open doorway. The girl gestured for me to enter and I stepped into a large area furnished with a single bed and some battered, second-hand furniture.

Dumping my rucksack onto the bed, I turned to find that the girl was gone and the ghostly patter of her descending footsteps echoed hollowly from the stairway.

I shrugged and approached the windows. Down on Rue Littré, street lamps shuddered in the strengthening breeze. A solitary individual in a heavy overcoat appeared to be performing an erratic dance in the middle of the footpath until I realised that he was, in fact, struggling to remain upright against the wind.

Sitting on the bed, I pulled two needles, a ball of wool and a length of rope from my bag. Strapping my ankle to the leg of the bed, I started to knit.

At midnight it started to snow.

Despite my fatigue I didn't sleep. The train journey from Paris had exacerbated my mangled sleeping patterns, and my body was struggling to determine whether it should be awake or asleep, or both.

It was still dark when my alarm clock rang at seven the following morning. I washed, dressed and stumbled downstairs to the first floor, where I found a communal kitchen that smelled strongly of yeast. I was staring out at the gloomy rooftops of Wazemmes when a dust-covered telephone on a shelf beside the fridge began to ring. I lifted the receiver.

"*Allo?*"

"*Dia dhuit, a Donnacha!*"

The voice was husky, female and laced with a familiar Donegal accent. My fist tightened around the phone and it was, suddenly, very hard to breathe.

"Nuala!"

"*Is é mise.*" It's me.

Her Gaelic resonated down the telephone wire, slipping into my ear and into my soul. I was too shocked, too shaken, to frame any kind of response.

"You're not in Paris," she said.

"I ... I don't work there any more. I resigned and left the flat last week."

A surprised grunt settled into the growing silence. "Why? You always wanted to live in some exotic foreign city like Paris."

"It seemed like the right thing to do."

There was a pause at the other end of the line as she considered this.

"So what are you doing in Lille?"

"Sleepwalking."

She laughed — a dry chuckle like dead leaves being swept along a pavement.

"Really?"

"Really. I've had problems sleeping for the last few months. Lately things have deteriorated to the point where I'm sleepwalking regularly. Now, if I fall asleep in one place — even in the middle of the day — I wake up somewhere else without any recollection of how I got there. My doctor thought it sufficiently serious to organise an appointment with a specialist on sleep disorders here in Lille."

"Forgive me for saying so, but that sounds hard to believe."

"No harder than talking to you."

My heart twisted then and something broke inside.

"This is crazy. I should hang up."

But I didn't.

"I wish you'd stayed in Paris," I whispered.

Several seconds passed before Nuala responded.

"Living in a foreign country's fine when everything's fresh and new, but eventually you end up missing the familiar: your own home, your culture, your language. That absence tends to make a hole you have to fill." She paused. "It was time for me to go home, Donnacha."

There wasn't much I could say to that. Raised on the Donegal coast,

Nuala was a woman of harsh landscapes and rugged coastlines. Despite years of travel, she'd felt stifled by the restrictive brickwork, the narrow streets and dogshit of central Paris. It had been a struggle for her to balance her affection for me with a conflicting desire to return to the life she'd left in Ireland.

"I still don't understand why you decided to leave."

"Because I missed you," I said simply.

Nuala sighed.

"God, we're a sad pair of bastards!"

A leaden torpor held me in the kitchen long after I'd hung up and I sat there fingering a blue woollen scarf, the last present I'd received from Nuala, one that she had knitted especially for me.

I was still sitting there when a thin young man in a ragged T-shirt and underpants stumbled through the doorway, absently scratching his balls. Oblivious to my presence, he lurched towards the sink and poured a glass of water. When he'd finished drinking it, he put it aside and returned the way he'd come, this time scratching his ass. He halted abruptly when he saw me.

"*Salut!*" I said.

A bewildered expression passed over his face as beleaguered, half-fried thoughts struggled to make sense of my appearance.

"Who the fuck are you?" he exclaimed at last in a heavy New Zealand accent.

"I'm Donnacha."

We eyed each other coolly. Finally he shrugged.

"I'm Ray," he said. "Let's have a smoke."

The walls of Ray's room were papered with a diverse collection of heavy metal posters and a large reproduction of the New Zealand flag. The floor was strewn with discarded clothing and some psychedelically coloured beanbags. Following his lead, I folded into the nearest one and watched as he proceeded to roll a joint. I glanced at the open doorway.

"You're not concerned someone will complain to the landlord?"

"Nah, mate! Most of the other tenants are dope-heads too. Besides, nobody's ever seen the landlord."

"Why not?"

He grinned. "Because he's never been here. I reckon he's just some long-term investor who's never even been to Wazemmes. The agency handles the rent and administration." He glanced up at me. "I assume that's how you're here?"

I nodded.

He shrugged as though he'd made his point and lit the completed joint. "I've been staying here for the last year. I'm working in a bar and teaching English until I save enough money to carry on travelling again.

He leaned over and passed me the spliff. "What do you do, then?"

"I used to be a translator in Paris — mostly English to Spanish — but I resigned last week. I'm staying here until I figure out what I'm going to do next."

"You're spending Christmas *here*!" Ray stared at me incredulously.

"I'm not really up to a Christmas with friends or family at the moment."

"Don't you have a girlfriend or something?"

"Split up six months ago. She was homesick and went back to Ireland."

"Ah, yeah! I can understand that. I hang out with some other expats but it's not the same as being at home. Most of us seem to come together because of our differences to the French, rather than similarities between ourselves."

"Are there others living here?"

Ray held up a pair of fingers. "Just two at the moment. Me and Monique. The others have already left for Christmas."

Monique, I assumed, would be the girl at the front door from the previous night, but the reference to Christmas caught me by surprise. I vaguely recalled colourful neon blurs strung across the streets the night before but I'd been so tired that they hadn't really registered.

There was a knock at the door and I looked up to see the girl in the doorway. She blinked when she saw me then quickly turned to Ray.

"*T'as du shit, Ray?*"

He waved her in and she settled into another beanbag, nonchalantly accepting the proffered joint. I watched as she inhaled, dragging the smoke deep into her lungs then releasing it slowly through her nose.

"Monique has a nose for shit," said Ray.

"*Putain de baba cool!*" she laughed — a surprisingly high-pitched chime that floated through the room like the tinkle of champagne glasses. She reached out and plucked a woollen jersey from the floor.

"Can I have this?" she asked Ray.

"Sorry, Monique. It's freezing outside. I need it myself."

Before she could respond a muffled buzzing emanated from Ray's bed.

"'Scuse me!"

Ray pulled a mobile phone from beneath the pillow and hurried from the room.

"Business call," explained Monique. "His dope supplier."

"Ah!"

Monique and I continued to smoke in silence. In the background Ray's voice drifted up from the kitchen like the muted drone of a priest at an interminable church service. When the roach had burned down, she stubbed it out and scrutinised me with an evaluative eye.

"Are you going to make a move on me then?"

I scratched the stubble on my chin.

"No. You're safe. I have a girlfriend."

"Fidelity!" she exclaimed. "How commendable! Do you have a photograph?"

I extracted a crumpled photo from my wallet and handed it to her. She considered it carefully for several seconds.

"What's her name?"

"Nuala."

"Nool-ah." She repeated the name, rolling the syllables around her mouth to see how it sounded.

"She's very beautiful. You're right. I am going to be safe with you."

I didn't answer. I'd just looked outside.

It had stopped snowing.

At eight-thirty, I left Ray and Monique to settle in with a freshly-rolled joint and let myself out through the front door. Rue Manuel was glazed with a thick coating of snow — a pristine whiteness that flowed between the buildings and blunted sharp corners with soft, rounded edges. There were no footprints, no tyre treads, no marks of any kind. Nothing but a bleached crystal gleam that scorched my eyeballs.

Numb from the effects of the drug and a growing migraine buzz, I took the metro to the centre of town and proceeded on foot to Rue Nationale and the address I was seeking. The building turned out to be an up-market office block with a grand marble entrance. '*Clinique Dr Roux*' was located through a large double door on the ground floor. When I entered, a smartly dressed woman behind the reception desk was comparing a half-completed cardigan with a knitting pattern from a womens magazine.

"*Bonjour!*"

Startled, the woman stuffed her wool and needles beneath the counter.

"*Monsieur.*"

"My name is Breathnach. I have a nine o'clock appointment with Dr Roux."

Struggling to regain her composure, the receptionist consulted the appointments register.

"I'm sorry, *Monsieur*. All appointments for the week were rescheduled due to technical difficulties with our computer system. Your appointment ..." she checked the screen "... was rescheduled for after Christmas. According to our records, a notification was sent to your address in Paris last week."

I closed my eyes, and the fatigue I'd been resisting for so long dropped onto my shoulders like a dead weight, threatening to knock me to the floor.

"Look, I've just changed address, so I didn't get your note. I've also come quite a long way to make this appointment."

"I'm afraid Doctor Roux is extremely busy."

"Isn't there any way you could fit me in?"

She hesitated, pursed her lips and appeared to relent. "Our policy does permit us to accept alternative appointments if we receive a cancellation before noon, but it's impossible to tell if someone will cancel, particularly so close to the holidays." She shrugged. "You're welcome to wait, of course."

"Very well."

"Pardon?" She peered over the rim of her spectacles.

"I'll wait."

"Oh."

She gestured loosely to a set of chairs on the far side of the room. "Very well. *Veuillez patientez, Monsieur.*"

A growing weariness settled over me as I awaited the unlikely chance of a cancelled appointment. Time passed slowly, dragging due the lack of any meaningful distraction within the featureless confines of the reception area. There were no magazines, no windows, and even the receptionist did little more than type sporadically on her computer or surreptitiously work on her knitting beneath the counter.

After what seemed like an hour, the door to the clinic opened abruptly. I glanced up with interest as a tall man in a pair of striped pyjamas and dressing gown strode into the room. He smiled broadly at the receptionist, who ignored him, then approached the chairs and sat down beside me.

"Hallo," he said politely. "What are you in for, then?"

"I sleepwalk."

"No shit!" He looked at me with interest. "That must be interesting."

"Not really." I regarded his pyjamas curiously. "What about you?"

"Dream anxiety."

"Dream anxiety?"

"Yes. Sometimes my dreams are so realistic I can't work out whether

I'm awake or asleep. Take this conversation, for example. It's quite possible you're nothing more than a figment of my imagination."

He removed a handkerchief from the pocket of his dressing gown and blew his nose.

"It's not only that! What's worse is that when I wake up I can't be sure whether I'm awake or simply dreaming that I'm awake. It's all very frustrating! And then of course, if it is a dream, there's the issue of knowing how much relevance to attach to it. It all comes down to personal opinion in the end, but everyone has their own pet theory. Some people say dreams are a reflection of the soul, some say they're nothing more that a kaleidoscopic clutter of blurred fantasies and memories." He held out his hands and grinned helplessly. "Who's to know?"

"*Monsieur!*"

"Hmm..?"

Startled, I turned to find the receptionist glaring at me, the shrill echo of her voice still hanging faintly in the air. My eyes flickered to the clock on the wall behind her. It was twelve o'clock, almost three hours since my arrival. Turning to my right, I discovered that the chair beside me was empty.

Shaken, I rose and approached the receptionist who'd folded her hands together in a no-nonsense, business-like manner.

"Unfortunately, Monsieur, no cancellations have been received and Dr Roux is fully committed for the remainder of the day."

Turning away, she focused her attention on her knitting and pointedly ignored me. Confused, I lingered uncertainly at the counter, then leaned over and pointed at the half completed cardigan.

"You've missed a stitch," I said.

I returned to Rue Manuel that afternoon to find a white van parked on the kerb outside the boarding house. The vehicle was surrounded by a number of Algerian labourers who were arguing and gesticulating animatedly over a set of street plans. Too weary to even question the reason for their presence, I slipped past and entered the building behind them.

I spent the rest of the afternoon on my bed in a somnolent paralysis, vaguely conscious of the shadows moving across the wall like some inexorable, undefined threat. I must have fallen asleep at some stage without noticing, for I was suddenly aware that it was dark. Feeling an odd chill around my eyes, I raised my hands to my face and discovered that they were full of tears. I had been crying in my sleep.

To revive my fragile morale I made a pot of tea down in the kitchen and sipped the bitter-tasting beverage while sitting at the battered table. The room felt wrong — all awkward angles and uncomfortable shadows — so I switched off the light and sat in the darkness. My eyes fell on the telephone, which someone had replaced to its original position on the shelf. Suddenly it erupted into life, its high-pitched ring violently stirring the silence from the room.

"Hallo?"

"*Is é mise arís.*" It's me again.

"*A Nuala!*"

I sighed. I'd almost convinced myself that I'd imagined our previous conversation.

"*Tá tu sa chathair fós!*" You're still in the city!

"Yes."

"I don't miss the cities. The first thing I did when I got back to Ireland was to head for the country and the coastline near my parents' house. I must have spent hours there just watching the seals on the rocks, smelling the gorse on the wind …

I sank into the darkness and allowed her voice to wash over me, imagining that she was there beside me, murmuring quietly in my ear. It was only as I listened to her that I realised how much I'd missed speaking Gaelic, how much the language linked us in a way that no other language ever could. The truth was that when I spoke English or French or Spanish I was speaking with my head. When I spoke Gaelic, however, I was speaking from my heart. And, hence, the inevitable connection with Nuala.

"You should go home, Donnacha," she said, as though reading my mind.

"Maybe I should," I admitted. "But, to be honest, I'm not sure where home is any more. You know what it's like when you try to fit back in after living overseas. The longer you leave it, the harder it gets."

"It doesn't really matter, Donnacha. At the end of the day, home is where the heart is."

"Well, Nuala, then I'm kind of fucked, aren't I?"

Sometime before ten o'clock the front door creaked open and someone climbed the stairs to the first floor. There was a soft click and the kitchen exploded in brightness.

"Christ!" yelled Ray. "What the fuck are you doing here?"

"Sitting."

"Mate, you seem to be making a habit of hanging around the kitchen scaring the shit out of me."

I considered that for a moment.

"Tea?" I suggested.

Ray was in an odd humour. Initially unenthusiastic and reluctant to talk, he livened up dramatically when it came to discussing the subject of his home, New Zealand. For over twenty minutes I listened dutifully without interruption as he expounded on the beauty of the snow-capped Mt Taranaki, and the rivers and heartland of the countryside, in painstaking detail. He spoke passionately, longingly, much in the same way that Nuala had spoken of Donegal before she left.

Ray stopped in mid-sentence as he caught sight of the wool and needles I was gathering up from the chair beside me. A male with knitting materials was clearly a foreign concept.

"Mate," he queried anxiously, "you're not gay, are you?"

I shook my head.

"Take it easy, Ray. My girlfriend taught me. It relaxes me."

"What are you knitting?"

"A car."

"You should knit a new girlfriend."

He chuckled heartily, considerably amused by his own wit.

"Ray," I asked. "What's the story with the phone?"

"Aaah! That phone's been bust since I've been here. All you get is static or weird noises. One of the previous tenants told me it didn't work when he first lived here and that was years ago. That's the real problem with absentee landlords. Nothing ever gets bloody fixed!"

He sipped some tea and grimaced.

"Nowadays, I just use a mobile. You should get one."

"I don't like them. I had one in Paris but people kept ringing me on it."

The rattle of the front door distracted us from the topic of telephones. We listened to the rapid tattoo of footsteps on the stairs and a moment later Monique entered the kitchen with two blank painting canvases under her arm. She nodded brusquely as she poured herself a glass of milk from the fridge.

"*Salut, les gars!*"

Swallowing the contents in a single gulp, she wiped her lips with the back of her hand and, tilting her head in a dismissive gesture, left the room.

Ray watched her go and shook his head.

"French chicks, eh!"

He turned to me.

"She's an artist, you know. She paints stuff."

"Is she any good?"

He looked at me blankly. "She uses lots of colours," he hazarded at last.

Our conversation faded shortly afterwards and Ray and I retired to our rooms. I was preparing to go to bed when there was a soft knock on the door.

"*C'est Monique!*"

I quickly concealed the rope.

"Come in."

The door opened and Monique silently slipped inside.

"I need to borrow a book. Do you have any books?"

Without waiting for a response, she moved to the single desk and rummaged through the books and papers I'd piled there. After a moment or two she held up a copy of Muiris Ó Súilleabháin's *Fiche Bliain Ag Fás*.

"Can I have this?"

"Can you read Gaelic?"

"No."

It seemed such a bizarre request that I wasn't sure how to respond. I settled for an ambiguous silence and after a moment she put the book aside and seemed to forget about it.

"Your girlfriend," she declared in an abrupt change of topic, "she can't be very good."

"Why do you say that?"

"She's not here to take care of you."

"No."

"I suppose she has a good reason."

"Uh-huh."

"Maybe it's because you split up." A sardonic grin curled up from the corner of her mouth. "You need to watch Ray. He's a bit of a gossip." She clicked her tongue and studied me closely. "So did she dump you first or did you dump her?"

I glared at her.

"Ah. That would have been her, then." She headed for the door. "I hadn't realised you Irish were such a romantic race."

"Ah, yes. Major romantics, us Gaels."

She stopped and turned to peer at me curiously.

"You're a strange person."

I didn't respond to that, but coming from Monique I felt it was pretty rich.

That night I repeated my night-time ritual of securing my foot to the leg of the bed, then leaning against the wall until oblivion hit me. Despite my precautions, however, early the following morning I became aware of a sharp burning sensation in the soles of my feet and shuddered awake to find myself standing barefoot in the snow in the centre of Rue Manuel.

"Ah, for fuck's sake!"

Cursing furiously, I retreated to the dim rectangle of light that marked the doorway of the boarding house. I was shivering violently by the time I got back to my room and the welcome warmth of my duvet. Too shaken to attempt sleep again, I remained in a state of semi-conscious exhaustion until I was jolted awake by the sound of the other tenants leaving and banging the front door behind them.

It was a struggle to leave my bed again but I somehow managed to get up, dress and catch a metro back into the city centre before nine o'clock. The receptionist at 'Clinique Dr Roux' was clearly surprised to see me back again. She greeted me with frosty cordiality but was openly disgruntled when I settled into the chair I'd occupied the previous day.

This time, to prevent myself falling asleep, I repeatedly pricked myself in the thigh with a drawing pin I'd brought along specifically for that purpose. It hurt and by midday my thighs were bleeding freely in several spots but at least I was still awake when the receptionist finally called me to the desk and confirmed that no cancellations had been received.

She smiled widely but you could tell it was an effort. "Do you have a phone number, *Monsieur*? We can contact you if we have a cancellation. It would save you coming in every morning."

"I'm afraid not," I replied.

Fissures appeared in the professional composure.

"But surely you have better things to do?"

I thought about that for several seconds.

"Not really."

Gritting her teeth, the receptionist typed intently for a second, then turned to look at me in disapproval.

"I have just booked an appointment with Dr Roux for nine o'clock tomorrow. Please try to be on time.

"See you tomorrow," I smiled.

The temperature plummeted again that afternoon and the sky stretched like a tight grey canvas over the buildings on either side of Rue Manuel. Outside the boarding house, the Algerian workmen had completed several large holes over two metres deep, and the snow around them had been churned up into a soft brown sludge.

I watched the Algerians at work from the kitchen window as I sipped a fresh cup of tea and observed how, in the freezing air, the warm breath rising from the holes resembled steam from a volcanic crater.

I was still watching them when a wave of weariness struck, knocking me so violently that the cup tumbled from my hand. Struggling to my feet, I tried to make it to the door but the shadows rushing in from my peripheral vision were too thick and too fast. There was one frightening moment of vertigo, then I fell headlong into a dark, endless tumble.

The first physical sensation I became aware of was heat: a luxurious all-encompassing warmth that drew me deep towards its source. After the perception and recognition of heat came another sensation — the smoothness of skin against skin.

My eyes flicked open.

"Hallo," said Monique.

I considered the cool green eyes and snub nose that lay less than three inches from my own. Beneath the duvet I could feel her breasts pressing firmly against my ribs.

"Hallo."

"How are you feeling?"

"I'm not sure," I answered carefully. "How about you?"

"Oh, I'm good," she confirmed. "Very comfortable, thank you."

I coughed.

"What are you doing in my bed?"

"I'm not in your bed. You're in my bed."

I raised my head and looked around. Sure enough, despite the gloom, I was able to make out several unfamiliar items of furniture and a number of paintings hanging from the walls.

Monique twisted onto her back, an action that moved her breasts away but brought her hip sliding up alongside my own.

"I was painting here yesterday afternoon when you came in without knocking. I asked you what you wanted but you ignored me, undressed, climbed into my bed and fell asleep. I left you alone until eleven o'clock, but then I was tired so I got in as well."

She gestured at a digital clock on the bedside table whose fluorescent numbers read 05:15. "You've been asleep for almost seventeen hours."

"Did we …?"

She chuckled quietly and snuggled back to her side of the narrow mattress.

"No, but earlier this morning you called me Nuala and hugged me. I think you were too tired to have sex." She sniffed and rubbed her nose. "We can try later, if you like."

"I think … I think I'm still a bit tired. But thank you."

"That's okay. I'm tired too. I'm not used to having visitors."

"I should probably go back to my own bed and let you rest." I reached down to the floor and groped around where my clothes lay scattered around my backpack.

"Have you seen my boxers?"

She yawned.

"I'm wearing them."

I stared at her.

"Why are you wearing my boxers?"

"I was cold."

"Oh." The logic of that response temporarily eluded me, but given the circumstances I decided not to argue the point.

I climbed out of bed and gathered up the backpack and the remaining items of clothing that I was able to locate. When I was dressed I removed a small package wrapped in newspaper from my backpack and handed it to Monique. "Here."

"What's this?"

"A present to say thanks for letting me sleep, for letting me sleep so long in your bed."

Rubbing her eyes, Monique sat up, unfolded the paper and pulled out a pair of hand-knitted socks.

"They're different colours."

40

"I didn't think you'd mind. Besides, you already have my boxers."
She mused on that briefly.
"Fair enough."
She lay down and turned away towards the wall.
"Goodbye, Donnacha."
I stood up to go.
"Goodbye, Monique."
Just as I reached the door, she called after me.
"Donnacha, can I ask you for a favour?"
"Sure."
"If you do feel like trying later, can you talk dirty to me in Gaelic?"

※

When I left Monique I didn't return to my own bedroom, but descended to the chilly murkiness of the deserted kitchen. Switching on the electric heater, I made a pot of tea and placed the telephone on the table in front of me. I was just about to sip my tea when Ray startled me by arriving in the kitchen.

"I bloody knew you'd be here!" he said, dropping a heavy rucksack to the floor. "Merry Christmas."

"What?"

"It's Christmas Eve." He regarded in surprise. "Christmas! I'm off to catch the ferry to England. I'm spending the holidays with some mates in London."

"Oh."

"What are you doing with the phone?"

"Nothing."

"That's good," said Ray. "You realize you won't get any dial tone. The telephone company's been working on the lines in this street for the last few days but they haven't finished repairing them yet."

I looked at him blankly.

"Hadn't you noticed them — a bunch of Algerians with a white van?"

"I haven't noticed much over the last few weeks," I admitted.
Ray poured himself a bowl of cereal and joined me at the table.
"I've got a question for you," he said. "A translation question."
"Yeah?"
"What's the Irish for 'fucking'?"
I looked at him in bewilderment.
"*Ag bualadh craiceann.* Literally, beating or smacking skin. Why?"
"Are you and Monique *ag bualadh craiceann*?"
He continued to scrutinise me closely.
"No."
He chewed thoughtfully on a crust of baguette.
"I heard you in her room last night and I've got to admit I'm a bit pissed. I've been trying to get it on with Monique for the last ten months. I was just starting to make some serious progress until you arrived and screwed things up."
"Ray, I haven't screwed anything up but believe me when I say you weren't making progress."
Ray stared wordlessly at the table for almost a minute.
"Yeah, I know," he said at last.
We both ate without speaking and the kitchen echoed to the sound of crackling cereal.
"God, I miss home!" sighed Ray.
"Yeah," I said. "I guess, I know what you mean."

When Ray left to catch his lift to Dunkerque, I remained by the telephone and waited. As anticipated, the high-pitched ring reverberated around the kitchen within seconds of Ray's departure.
"*Dia dhuit, a Donnacha.*"
"*A Nuala.*"
"Is it late or is it early?"
"I suppose it doesn't really make much difference."
There was a long, intense silence.
"What is it, Donnacha?" she asked.

"It's kind of hard to say."

"Try."

I stared out at the early morning gloom. In the distance, dark shapes flitted against the bright rectangles of windows in neighboring buildings as their inhabitants rose and prepared for a new day.

"Two months after you returned to Ireland. You were in a car accident." I paused, struggling for the words. "There weren't any survivors, *mo chroí*."

"Yes, I know!"

A cold gust of wind rattled the window panes and out in the darkness an alley cat yowled.

"So you realise its time to let me go, Donnacha."

"I'm sorry, Nuala. I hadn't understood, I hadn't realised …"

My voice trailed off, absorbed into the silence of the empty kitchen.

"Tell me about the funeral," she urged.

"A rainy day up on the clifftop cemetery. Black rain on black umbrellas. Black clothes, black rock. Everyone was cold and miserable. Everything felt sad and dead and broken."

"And you, Donnacha?"

"I couldn't feel anything, Nuala. I couldn't feel anything."

"Then I'm sorry too, Donnacha."

"What are you sorry for? You're the one who died."

"I'm sorry I left you all alone."

She sighed.

"You have to mourn now, Donnacha. To sit quietly and release me in little pieces as far as you can. But when I'm gone, please don't forget me." There was a choking, strangled sound. "*Slán leat, mo chroí!*" Goodbye my love.

Although nothing in the room had changed, I had the strangest impression that Nuala had somehow, receded from me. For several seconds I was sure I could hear her breathing, then even this seemed to fade away, swallowed up by the sound of an eerie wind keening down the line.

"Nuala!" I called, but there was no reply. The phone went dead.

It took me less than twenty minutes to pack. When I stepped out onto Rue Manuel I found that a fresh layer of snow had smothered the street — deep and crisp and even — and the world was, once again, shiny and new.

Wrapping Nuala's scarf around my neck, I walked towards the metro.

And started to let her go.

After the beep

BEEEEPP!

Do you know what the irony is, Frank? The irony is that I'm sitting here in the dark, justifying myself to an answerphone with a message you'll probably never receive.

If you do get this message, your first thought might be to wonder why I'm calling. Why am I sitting in a darkened room baring my soul to the metallic void of an indifferent recording device?

A sensible question, I'd have to concede.

If you do have a moment to learn a little more about this particular debacle, you'd have to be prepared go back to the beginning to fully understand it.

Let me tell you about that, Frank.

Do you have a moment?

It all began less than five months ago. On April 14th, to be precise. Does that date ring any bells with you, Frank? Anything about ships? Icebergs, perhaps?

Typical of most cataclysms, it wasn't instigated by an event of any particular importance but by a series of independently escalating incidents; trivial things that, by themselves, could hardly be considered significant.

Take the first such incident, for example. A deceptively innocuous sentence — a single line on the Telecomstra telecommunications invoice I received on the 14th of April. It read:

High speed internet access – $45.

Even at the time I couldn't help but be intrigued by this particular sentence. As far as I could recall I hadn't registered for an internet service. Although I ran a small, home-based business making up agricultural compounds, it wasn't sufficiently successful to require a computer — not to mind an internet connection.

Needless to say, like any law-abiding citizen I picked up the phone to do my duty and clarify the matter. Back then, of course, I was still blissfully ignorant of the obstacles awaiting me, the recorded obstructions that would prove more daunting than anything I could have anticipated.

My initial attempt at clarification ended almost immediately with a beeping 'engaged' tone. Three later attempts were rewarded with similar results.

On my fifth attempt, I succeeded in bypassing the apparent mob of eager callers and got a ringing tone only to be confronted with a series of recorded options apathetically muttered by what sounded like a sedated zombie. "The options …" moaned this wretched individual, "are as follows. Press:

1. To sign up with Telecomstra services
2. To report a fault
3. To register for additional internet services
4. To hear about other Telecomstra products."

Unfortunately, as none of these options fitted my particular circumstances, I wandered the highways and byways of Telecomstra recordings for the next twenty minutes, following a trail of messages from option to option like some kind of magical thread through a fairytale forest. As the messages stretched on and on, I grew drowsy, slowly succumbing to the mesmerising influence of endless recordings. Faltering, I began to sink, deep into the hypnotic mire of telecommunication hell until a sudden, unexpected voice wrenched me irreverently from my stupor.

"Hallo?"

In that instant I experienced a rare moment of philanthropic connection with my fellow *homo sapiens*. For almost two full seconds

I truly felt at one with my brothers and sisters of humankind.

"Hallo! Please help me! Your company's billing me for a high-speed internet service. I don't have an internet connection! I don't even have a computer!"

"I'm sorry sir. This is the Mobile Billing department. You need to speak to the Landlines Billing department. Transferring you now."

"Wait!"

"Have a nice day."

An electronic hiss crackled in my ear for several seconds, then another phlegmatically ethereal voice wavered from the earpiece.

"This is Landline Accounts. All of our operators are currently occupied but your call has been placed in a priority queue. You will be connected with an operator as soon as one becomes available. Your call is important to us. Have a nice day."

Needless to say, nobody ever answered my call. I persevered on that line for another half hour, determined not to relinquish my place in the queue. I remained resolute, visualizing my progress as that of a tiny worm traversing a vast wasteland, slowly but inexorably wriggling towards its destination. Just when I was convinced that I was almost there, just as I was poised to reach out and grasp that prize, that holy grail of wriggling worms, another mumbled message rattled down the phone and into my ear like a rejected coin from a slot machine.

"This is Telecomstra. Your call has just exceeded the permissible time limit for incoming calls. In the interest of other callers your call will now be disconnected. To reconnect with Telecomstra or to discuss any difficulties you might be having please feel free to telephone us again or contact us through our internet website. Have a nice day."

Imagine that! Rejected on the whim of a two-bit piece of digital software! A third-rate mainframe with pretensions of grandeur!

I should have let it go, I suppose! I should have heeded the omens, the portents circling my soul like a flock of determined vultures. God knows I tried! I really tried! But every week another invoice would slip through my letterbox, threatening to terminate services unless there was prompt receipt of the overdue amount.

Four weeks later the threats were actually executed and my telephone line was disconnected, a disaster for a self-employed person working from home. My business began to fail as my clients, unable to contact me, began to drift away. Seeking an alternative telecommunications company, I discovered that none of them were willing to supply me. By some strange coincidence, I'd somehow been assigned a negative credit rating and was now designated a financial risk within the industry.

Desperate to salvage my livelihood, I continued in my attempts to contact a rational entity at Telecomstra but each time I was led astray by the myriad options (empty promises, Frank! Empty promises!), put on hold or simply disconnected. On one miraculous occasion, I actually came close. Following a sequence of options I'd not previously attempted I was astoundingly rewarded with instant acknowledgement from another human being.

"Hallo. Mobile Billing department."

"Oh God — not you again!"

"Excuse me."

"I'm terribly sorry. It's just that I've been trying for weeks to talk to someone about my telephone connection. I'm getting quite desperate."

"I'm sorry sir. This is the Mobile Billing department. You need to speak to the Landlines Billing department."

"Ah," I said, in my desperation resorting to a hitherto dormant animal cunning. "But Landlines Billing told me to speak to you."

The pause that followed was thick and menacing, laden with unexpressed threats of painful ramifications. As I waited, enveloped by that portentously deadly silence it was as though I could discern the operator's thoughts, the arguments and counterarguments, churning around in her head through a million miles of telecable. Suddenly;

"Transferring you now sir. Have a nice day."

"Wait!"

"This is Landline Accounts. All of our operators are currently occupied but your call has been placed in a priority queue. You will be connected with an operator as soon as one becomes available. Your call is important to us. Have a nice day."

Have I mentioned Deirdre, Frank?

Have I told you about that beautiful woman I've never had the opportunity to meet? Maybe I've spoken of her gentle tones, that musical Irish accent sliding down the phone like rich butter melting over wholegrain toast.

Let me tell you about Deirdre.

Eight weeks had passed since my initial enquiry. My business was on the verge of ruin as my clients disappeared to do business with those fortunate enough to have a functioning telephone line. Even at that late stage I was still trying to contact someone at Telecomstra, although I was now reduced to calling from pay phones or friends' apartments. I even went so far as 'borrowing' a mobile lying unattended at a café I frequented and in the relative safety of the café toilets used my new acquisition to make a fresh attempt at contacting Telecomstra. Erring on a complicated set of recorded options, however, an unexpected 'kink' in the operating system transferred me to the company head office. Stunned, I listened to an almost alien sound — a ringing tone.

"Hallo, Telecomstra. This is Deirdre speaking."

When I heard that voice, Frank, it was like a balm, a calming sound that rolled down through the telephone wire to sooth my troubled soul. I knew then that I was talking to an angel. I'd somehow obtained a direct line to God and for one precious moment it was as though all that effort and stress had actually been worthwhile. Deirdre was a voice with a real human being attached. She radiated warmth and genuine concern — a far cry from the automated mutterings of the recorded voices.

Over the next six weeks, Deirdre was my guide through the telecommunication wilderness. Over that period, she worked with me, encouraged me, murmuring patiently as she led me through each option, then cursing conspiratorially each time we encountered a fresh obstacle. Deirdre even did what no one else had offered to do — she would ring me back — usually at isolated telephone booths or a quiet café with a public telephone from where we could discuss our latest strategy.

Deirdre spent weeks trying to remove my name from Telecomstra's list of internet users and although her efforts achieved little more than replacing the relevant line on my invoice with a different colour it never really mattered because I loved her for trying, just for trying. You see, we connected, Frank! We truly connected!

Deirdre's daily call became the highlight of my day. Although a solitary person by nature, I found that I enjoyed talking to Deirdre and it was never a trial to wait in the rain next to a solitary telephone booth for her next call.

Until the day she didn't ring.

I instinctively knew that something was wrong although I didn't want to admit it at first. Despite my increasing sense of panic, I succeeded in remaining patiently at the telephone booth for two full hours before stumbling away in despair. Lacking cash to use a telephone booth or the funds to procure some change, I broke into the flat of a neighbour who'd recently gone away on holiday and threw myself on his telephone. My fingers fumbled over the numbers of Deirdre's direct dial but I finally managed to obtain a ringing tone. A moment later it was answered by a cool, distant voice I'd not encountered before.

"Deirdre who? Oh yes, the Irish girl. Gone in the latest restructure, I'm afraid. So sorry."

I have to admit that it all became something of an obsession for me at that point, Frank. As far as I was concerned, you'd destroyed my life. You'd reduced me to a quivering wreck but more importantly, you'd taken Deirdre away from me, something I knew I could never forgive. My hatred for Telecomstra intensified over the following weeks. At night I took to walking the streets, breaking into the homes of people who had telephones that actually worked. As they snored upstairs I'd sit in the darkness of their living rooms, feverishly pressing out options on their telephones like a chronic gambler before a one-armed bandit.

But all in vain!

All in vain!

It took me another two months to figure it out but I finally understood. I wasn't going to get anywhere through the consumer service lines. Corporate telecommunication systems are not set up to help consumers — they're set up to misdirect them, to lose them in the abyss, to prevent them from asking irritating questions. If I wanted to make any progress I had no option but to go directly to the top.

In the end, all it took was a single visit to the library — a quick flip through the register of companies and there it was — the names, titles and telephone numbers of the corporate office missing from all other official company literature. That's where I found out about you, Frank! Chief executive, major stakeholder, and original founder of the company. What an important fellow you must be! It's no wonder you resent being interrupted! Even your secretary seemed to think you were too important to be disturbed. She refused to pass me through until I convinced her it was an urgent personal call.

And so, Frank, to come full circle and return to my original question — do you know what the real irony is? I'm talking the true absurdity here, of course. Not the tacky, second-rate variety you can pick up for a dollar-fifty at the nearest discount shop.

Well, listen closely, Frank! Bolt the door of your office, pull the curtains, cup your hands around the earpiece so nobody else can listen while I whisper this in your ear.

The real irony, Frank, is that for a giant, all encompassing communications company — you guys couldn't communicate to save yourselves.

And there you have it! In the end that's the straw that broke this camel's back.

That's why I've broken into your house this evening. That's why I'm whispering to your faithfully recording electronic vacuum. That's also why I drove down to your head office last night and parked my van in your basement. By the way, the van's loaded with agricultural compounds — surprisingly explosive when mixed in the appropriate quantities.

I had the van primed to explode fifty minutes after commencing this call because I had all these great intentions of giving you and your staff enough warning to evacuate the building. Unfortunately, it's taken me forty minutes to navigate your labyrinthine telephone systems (options one to twelve, transfer, put on hold — you know the story) and even that's been in vain as I've been directed to nothing more than a recorded message informing me that you're currently in a meeting.

Oh well!

In any case, I do hope you finish your meeting and get a chance to check your messages so you can appreciate this final piece of irony.

Take care, Frank — oh and by the way!

Have a good day.

BEEEEPP!

The Ringmaster's Daughter

The magic was gone from the land. Of this much, at least, she was certain.

Winter scenes from the English countryside slid past the window of the railway carriage. Kathy Curtin considered the muddy brown fields and grim housing developments with a growing sense of melancholy. Although raised in a similarly bleak landscape on the western Irish coastline, there the lichen-coated standing stones and castle ruins had imbued the land with a resonance that softened its epidermal chill. This English countryside, however, was alien to her. She had no tie to this land, no cultural, historical or sympathetic connection linking her soul to the stones beneath the earth.

Your attention please! This train will shortly be arriving in Hove. Thank you.

The train's intercom delivered the announcement with a detached professionalism as cool as the windowpane. Relieved to be nearing her destination, Kathy pressed her face against the window. In the distance, where the coast was sliding into view, an enormous slab of cloud filled the horizon like a giant wave poised to break down on the land.

As they drew closer to the coast, the cloud continued to swell, bunching up like enormous lumps of cotton wool. Without warning, the train penetrated the cloud and there was a collective gasp from the passengers as they found themselves sliding through a landscape that was grey and frighteningly insubstantial. Beyond the window nothing was visible and if it hadn't been for the roll of the carriage they could have thought themselves simply standing still.

At that precise moment Kathy experienced a tremor of apprehension.

Maybe I am, she thought. Maybe I am just standing still.

Everything ended five metres from the doorway of the railway station. There, the substantial brickwork softened and faded into the ethereal as the mist dissolved everything it touched. Staring at the endless grey, Kathy experienced an inexplicable yearning to fling herself into it. Leaving the building, she plunged forward into the haze and as she ran she had the oddest impression of falling, as though plummeting earthwards through a cloud layer at 20,000 feet.

Exhausted but exhilarated, she slowed to a halt as the fog tightened in around her. The sound of breaking waves was loud in her ears but the sea was obscured from sight.

The words 'Tea-Room' flared magically out of the gloom a short distance from where she was standing. Approaching the glowing letters, she discovered its source — the flickering signage of a run-down café. Entering via a squeaking door, she ordered coffee from a yawning attendant and took a chair by the window. The coffee cup warmed her hands as she regarded the breadcrumbs on the floor and the cup rings burned into the formica table like a warped Olympic symbol.

Mist streamed past her window as she massaged a growing emptiness beneath her breast, only vaguely aware of the café door opening and another customer entering. A woman's voice with an unfamiliar, guttural accent ordered coffee.

Kathy glanced up to regard the newcomer — an olive-skinned young woman in her late twenties — colourfully attired in a red jacket with tails, a blue neckerchief and bright yellow pants that tapered down inside a pair of wool-lined leather boots. The most prominent feature of her unusual ensemble, however, was the top hat cocked at a precarious angle to one side of her head.

The vivid costume was strikingly out of place in the drab café and she couldn't help but stare. The girl turned abruptly as though sensing the scrutiny, taking in Kathy's plaited copper hair, business suit and briefcase. Kathy felt uncharacteristically exposed beneath that gaze and realised that with her uptown corporate wear she probably looked just as much out of place in the deserted seaside resort.

When she'd received her coffee, the girl approached the table and stood there quietly like some misguided rainbow that had somehow blown ashore in Hove.

"My name …" she said at last "… is Dal. It means 'lucky-one'. Do you mind if I join you?"

Flustered by the assured self-introduction, Kathy gestured helplessly at an adjoining seat. The girl dropped a knapsack on the floor, then sat and removed her hat. Long, black ringlets bungy-jumped down each side of her face. She stretched out one olive-tanned hand and Kathy accepted the proffered palm. A collection of copper bangles encircling the girl's wrists clinked together as they shook, emphasising each shake.

"What's your name?"

"Kathy."

"What does that mean?"

"It's an old Gaelic word. It means the 'put-upon-one'."

There was a silence as the girl took that on board. Kathy watched as she considered it, chewing it over like an unfamiliar taste.

"It suits you," she said at last and they both laughed.

She lit a cigarette, holding it with an uncontrived awkwardness that somehow looked surprisingly cool.

"You have an interesting face. When I lived in Adjanistan I knew a girl with a face like yours. I treated her for depression."

"You're a doctor?" Kathy was genuinely surprised.

"In a manner of speaking. I suppose you could call me a witch-doctor."

"Forgive me," Kathy said slowly. "I've not met a witch-doctor before."

"That's understandable. We don't do house calls."

Kathy nodded and put her cup aside.

"How did it work out?"

"How did what work out?"

"Your patient. The girl."

"She married a prince and had three beautiful children. The last I heard they were still living in marital bliss. All in all, a successful treatment."

"Mmm," said Kathy.

Despite her initial apprehension, Kathy lingered for a second coffee, increasingly intrigued by her new companion. Although not beautiful in a conventional sense, Dal had an attractive face and the combination of her natural intensity and idiosyncratic costume compelled attention. More importantly, she was refreshingly, invigoratingly, original — a welcome antidote to the wearying company of Kathy's acquaintances in the city.

Kathy examined her furtively over the lip of her coffee cup.

"Where are you from, Dal?"

"Gyor. It's a city in Eastern Hungary. My mother was born there." She brushed an invisible piece of fluff from her jacket. "My father was English. I learned English at boarding school in London while his work took him around Europe."

"Oh. Was he a diplomat?"

"No. A ringmaster."

Kathy glanced at Dal's hat on the chair beside her.

"A circus ringmaster?"

"Yes." Dal exhaled a thin stream of cigarette smoke. "He was quite famous back in the seventies. He was a ringmaster but he also had a remarkably powerful voice. People would travel hundreds of miles to see him perform an act where he'd smash wine glasses by raising the pitch of his voice."

"I'd always thought that was an old maid's tale."

"No. It's true." Dal finished her coffee and stared at the cup. "Do you feel like something a little stronger? There's a bar up the street."

"It would dance on my tongue."

When they emerged from the café the coolness of the evening air hit them in a rush, enveloping them with all the headiness of a passionate kiss. Darkness had settled in over the mist and Kathy glanced at her watch, surprised to discover it was already six o'clock.

Dal wafted her hands slowly through the tendrils of mist. "What a strange fog!"

Kathy grinned. "When I was a kid back in Ireland, whenever there was a fog like this we'd say the fairies were attempting to remake the world."

Dal regarded her curiously. "A less complex explanation than most."

"Simpler times," said Kathy. "Simpler times."

The outer façade of 'The Dog's Bollox' was an unpleasant mix of damp brick and plastic, dominated by a sign with a crude depiction of a dog licking his testicles. The internal décor, a corny Polynesian theme of Hawaiian leis and plastic palm trees, appeared surreally obtuse given the weather outside.

Despite the early hour, several patrons were huddled around the beer taps at the far end of the counter. They watched with interest as the girls dropped their bags at a corner table.

Dal cleared her throat.

"I'm afraid I'm a bit short of sterling. Could you lend me ten pounds until I get some money changed?"

Kathy hesitated then pulled a £10 note from her wallet and handed it to Dal. Accepting it gratefully, Dal approached the counter, returning a moment later with two pints of lager.

"The pub doubles as a B&B. It's getting late so I've taken the liberty of booking us a room. I can cancel it if that doesn't suit you."

Kathy shook her head. "Beats going back out into that mist."

Dal removed her jacket. Underneath she was wearing a purple, open-necked shirt that would have looked ridiculous on anyone without her hair and complexion.

"Nice shirt."

Dal disdainfully twisted the material between thumb and forefinger. "A second-hand bargain. Not like your suit. What is it? Cashmere?"

"Yeah. I work for a firm that expects you to dress professionally, even if it costs half your salary."

She dipped a finger in her beer.

"So! You lived in Adjanistan."

"Yes. Initially, I was working on contract with an international humanitarian agency but I ended up staying longer when I became involved with one of the local tribesmen." Dal shrugged. "Things didn't work out. After a year I packed my bags and was just on the point of leaving when he hustled me back into the house. He tied me to the table for five days, claimed I'd bewitched him and told me he wasn't going to let me leave."

"Jesus! How did you escape?"

Dal considered her coolly and exhaled a cloud of smoke.

"Why, I charmed him, of course!"

<hr>

"And this, is an Elixir of Bravery."

Dal held the small vial up to the light so that Kathy could see its contents — a viscous, rose-tinted liquid.

"It generates a temporary sensation of bravado and a lack of inhibition that lasts for up to thirty hours. Side-effects are rare but include arrogance and an irrational fear of heights."

She replaced the vial in a wooden box intricately carved with Asian designs. The box had twenty-four receptacles, each holding a similar vial.

Dal held up a second vial.

"This is an Elixir of Compassion. If used correctly it can complement a person's humanity and sometimes acts as an antidote to selfish action."

Kathy glanced at a barmaid rubbing down the neighbouring tables then turned to examine the vial with a sceptical eye.

"Do these actually work? Surely the pharmaceutical companies would sell them if they worked."

Dal shook her head.

"They base their product range on conditions that offer the greatest potential for profit. These normally tend to be cosmetic products or treatments for symptoms of repetitive conditions as opposed to genuine cures."

She shook her head unhappily. "Internationally, the rates of neuroses and depression are increasing. Pharmaceutical companies have responded by increasing their production of medicines for impotence and weightloss."

Kathy stared at the labels on the vials.

"Beauty, Sentiment and Serenity, these are all qualities! How do you treat physical symptoms with these?"

"They're not intended to treat symptoms. They target the spiritual ailments that create the symptoms."

"Oh," said Kathy carefully. "That's very … innovative."

"We Hungarians are innovative people."

"*Jó estét.*"

They turned to stare at the barmaid, who had appeared beside them.

The barmaid blushed. "I'm sorry. I overheard you saying you were Hungarian. My grandmother was from Bucharest. She taught me how to say 'Good evening' in Magyar." She frowned. "I was sure I'd said it correctly!"

"I'm sorry." Dal replaced the box in her knapsack. "I never speak Magyar in England. Excuse me."

Rising from the table, she walked towards the women's toilet.

Shaking her head, the barmaid returned to the counter. Kathy watched Dal's departing form and thoughtfully sipped her beer.

Dal was pale when she returned. Black bags hung under her eyes like bloated, sleeping bats.

"Are you all right?" asked Kathy.

"Just a little tired. I think I must have left Bucharest too quickly."

"You live in Bucharest?"

"At the moment, I have a job there with the International Circus Festival."

"You're kidding! You work for the circus?"

Dal laughed, amused by Kathy's reaction. "I do some acrobatic performances, but I wouldn't be too impressed. Circus work is tougher than many other jobs I've done. There's a lot of travel, it doesn't pay well and most physical performers have a limited career life." She yawned. "To be honest, I'm tired of the gypsy lifestyle. I've seriously considered settling down with a regular nine-to-five job." She scratched her chin. "Actually, I hope I still have a job to go back to. I didn't give much notice when I left."

"What was the rush?"

"I had to come here for a funeral."

"Oh! I'm sorry. A friend of yours?"

Dal sniffed. And scratched her chin again.

"My father. He's being buried tomorrow."

"The ringmaster!"

"Yes."

Kathy stared at her blankly, incapable of even imagining what a ringmaster might possibly have died from. "I'm sorry," she said at last.

Dal shrugged.

"We weren't very close. He travelled a lot and I didn't really see much of him after my mother died. He retired here in the mid-'70s but by then I'd finished school and left England. I didn't hear from him again until two years ago when I received his hat in the mail." She tapped the rim of the top hat. "No letter, no note — just a hat in a box."

She reached into her knapsack and withdrew a hardcover notebook wrapped with red elastic. Removing the elastic, she placed the notebook on the table, flicked through several pages of neat handwriting and withdrew a wrinkled black and white photograph.

"These are my parents."

She handed Kathy a photo of a couple standing by a circus tent. The man was tall and handsome, but had a stern face and a severe walrus moustache that gave him an oddly sinister appearance. The woman, dressed in an acrobat's costume, was pretty and had extraordinarily dark eyes. Kathy couldn't help noting that neither of them particularly resembled her companion.

"You don't look like your Dad."

"I take more after my mother. She was a trapeze artist. She died when I was nine. Fell from the trapeze rig before a performance in Belgium."

"Ah." Kathy decided not to push the point, but returned the photograph.

Dal inserted it in her notebook.

"I guess I've always had circus in the blood."

"Uh-huh," said Kathy.

Dal regarded her closely.

"You don't believe me."

Kathy felt the entire day's travel settle like a burden upon her shoulders. Sighing, she put her glass aside and looked at Dal.

"So far, you've been a witch-doctor, a tribesman's lover, a circus performer and a ringmaster's daughter. To be honest, your stories strain the limits of credibility." She shook her head wearily. "Jesus, I'm not even sure you're Hungarian! You could just be some local nut putting on a funny accent!"

"I am Hungarian."

"Show me your passport."

"It's in a locker at the station."

"How convenient."

"It's true!"

Kathy shook her head and a heavy silence slowly settled between them. The murmur of other conversations grew louder, rustling through the bar room like leaves in a breeze.

"Show me your hand," Dal said suddenly.

"Why?" Kathy's expression was cynical. "You going to read my palm?"

"Yes."

Kathy looked at her uncertainly.

"Oh, what the hell."

She held out her hand and Dal examined it with the tips of her fingers.

"You're here because of a broken heart."

Startled, Kathy pulled her hand away. Dal laughed.

"Don't be surprised. Everyone has a broken heart. Conditions like this ..." she gestured at the weather outside, "... aggravate the condition."

Kathy considered her impassively, then a crooked smile moulded itself across her features.

"Actually, I came here because of the name. Hove sounded like a sanctuary, a safe place somewhere between 'home' and 'cove'." She laughed then but the laughter sounded surprisingly brittle.

"I have a boyfriend. He's not a bad man, but he ... he's got a temper. We've been trying to work things out but it never seems to get any better. I should have left him earlier, but ..."

She hesitated, then hitched up one side of her blouse to reveal a long, yellow bruise running across her left ribcage. Three smaller, older bruises were scattered below her breast.

"This morning, after the latest ... I was waiting for the train to work when I found an intercity ticket on the ground by my feet. God only knows who lost it or how it got there, but as soon as I read the name of the destination — Hove — I knew I had to jump on a train and get here."

She snorted.

"It's probably the only impulsive thing I've done in years. Needless to say, as soon as I got here I realised what a fool I'd been." She shook her head in disbelief. "I have a job, for Christ's sake! Responsibilities! People depend on me."

She sighed.

"I'll take the first train back tomorrow. Tell everyone I was sick. They'll be wondering where I've got to."

She looked up, surprised to find Dal regarding her with an expression that was disturbingly bleak.

"Don't be too hard on yourself." Dal spoke slowly, calmly, but there was a chill to her voice that was genuinely unnerving.

"Things happen, people happen, that can tear you up inside. Sure, it hurts but you can get over the wound if you're strong enough, or learn to forgive the person who did it to you."

She paused and in the ensuing silence Kathy had a distinct impression that Dal, having inadvertently revealed too much, was now retreating tortoise-like inside her shell. Conscious of the awkward lull she'd created, Dal grinned awkwardly.

"Sorry. That was probably a bit heavy."

"But true," Kathy admitted. "I suppose it's a risk you take with all relationships. It's probably inevitable that when two people sleep together their dreams become entangled and they forget their true desires."

Dal leaned forward and looked her directly in the eye.

"And you, Kathy? What were your desires?"

Disturbed by the intensity of that stare, Kathy averted her eyes, focusing her attention on the dregs at the bottom of her glass.

"Magic!" she said at last. "I want the magic back in my life."

"Then maybe you should just keep on travelling," said Dal.

Without waiting for a response, she rose from the table and walked towards the bar.

Surprised by this brusque departure, Kathy watched as Dal chatted with the barman, apparently oblivious to the consternation she'd caused. Her companion's words had unsettled her, she realised. Twisting in under her skin to stir up unfamiliar sensations that she was at a loss to comprehend.

Sighing, she glumly studied her reflection in the beer glass. The distorted image reminded her of a Halloween game from her childhood, a *Samhain* Eve tradition where local girls would attempt to draw up 'the fetch' of their future husbands with candle-lit reflections from opposing hand-mirrors.

She shook her head and looked out the window, recalling her comments to Dal as they left the beachfront café.

Simpler times.

It was true, she reflected. Her childhood had been a simpler time, full of pagan wonderment and enchantment that had somehow fallen away as she'd grown older. Modern life in all its complexity and overwhelming pragmatism had reduced the magic, trivialised it. And the world was a sadder, lesser place for it.

Kathy did not sleep well that night. Trapped in a web of straitjacket dreams, she surfaced to consciousness a disoriented and scratchy mess. Groaning, she opened her eyes. It was morning. Dal, already dressed, was watching her.

"Good morning."

Kathy blinked and wiped her eyes.

"Good morning."

"Kathy, would you come to the funeral this morning?"

She stared at Dal with wary, bloodshot eyes.

"You want me to go to your father's funeral?"

"Yes."

"The ringmaster?"

"Yes."

Kathy held her gaze for several seconds, studying Dal's solemn expression for any trace of duplicity. Her features were inscrutable, infuriatingly difficult to decipher. It was impossible to tell if she was in earnest, in jest or simply insane.

Too tired to argue, she nodded her assent. She turned away to the wall and closed her eyes, determined to eke out a few final moments of illusionary solitude beneath the sheets. The world and its associated complications, she reasoned, could endure her absence for just a few minutes longer.

Mist still smothered the streets when they emerged from the Dog's Bollox, but despite the lack of discernible landmarks Dal appeared to know where she was going. She led Kathy confidently through several fog-bound lanes, then up an increasingly steep series of streets that seemed to continue without end. Tired and irritable, Kathy was just on the point of protesting when they, suddenly and unexpectedly, emerged from the cloud.

Kathy looked around in surprise. They were on an isolated hilltop that protruded above the mist like a tiny island in a sea of ruffled pillows. The visible terrain, consisting of little more than fifty square metres of sloping grass, converged to a central plateau where a small cemetery was located.

Kathy followed Dal hesitantly as she approached the cemetery, circling a line of lichen-coated tombstones to an open grave where a funeral service was already under way. Three other people were present. One, an elderly priest reading aloud from a prayer book, glanced up suspiciously at their arrival but made no acknowledgement of their presence. Two other roughly dressed men were in the process of lowering a coffin into the grave.

Kathy took a position behind a large gravestone and tried to remain as unobtrusive as possible. She noted that there wasn't a single funeral wreath in sight.

The service was brief but oddly vacant of any personal details. As she listened to the priest's detached monotone, Kathy had the impression that the deceased was a stranger not only to her but everyone else present. Bewildered, she glanced at Dal, struggling with conflicting emotions of sympathy and suspicion.

The priest brought the ceremony to an abrupt close, shutting his prayer book and scuttling off as though late for another appointment. The two gravediggers set to work immediately, filling the grave from a nearby mound of earth. Working industriously, they completed their task and departed without a word.

Dal approached the grave and looked down at the freshly turned earth. For almost a full minute she stood there, swaying slightly in the rising breeze as the silence of the hill top filled the air around her. Without warning, she fell to her knees and released a keen — a long, anguished ululation that resounded into the surrounding clouds. Shaken by the outburst, Kathy clutched the nearby headstone. She stared with horrified eyes as the keen washed over her and for one terrible, endless moment, it seemed as though the world was too fragile to take the pain.

Too small to contain the anguish.

"Would you like to talk about it?" Kathy asked. The question was an effort for her. She was still shaken by the incident on the hilltop and the memory of Dal, knees down in the dirt, screaming her distress into the heavens burned in her mind.

Dal paused as she raised a glass to her lips. She was stretched the length of her bed back in their room at the Dog's Bollox, and the expression on her face suggested that the question had taken her by surprise.

"Of course not!" she said.

They drank without speaking, staring at the floorboards for several minutes.

"What will you do now?" asked Kathy.

"Cut my hair short. Wear sensible shoes. Run away from the circus."

Kathy glanced sideways to see if she was joking, but Dal didn't appear to be smiling.

"I owe you an apology. I didn't believe your stories. Not until …" she hesitated, struggling for words to describe the events on the hill. "… your father's grave," she concluded lamely.

"How were you to know? You don't know anything about me. Besides …" Dal grinned, "I could be some local nut putting on a funny accent."

Kathy smiled weakly while Dal refilled their glasses with the flask of vodka she'd pulled from her bag.

"It was a pauper's funeral. He died penniless and without friends, hardly a pleasant conclusion to one's existence."

Kathy regarded her curiously.

"Jesus! You speak of him so dispassionately!"

Dal considered that for a moment.

"Yes. I understand you might find that odd but the truth is we were almost strangers." She tapped her glass with her finger. "We were closer when I was a child. Back then I used to think he was the strongest man in the world." She shrugged. "Now that I'm older and eminently more street-wise, I understand he was never really strong at all."

Kathy rolled the vodka around in her mouth, appreciating the burning sensation it left inside her cheeks.

"Maybe it wasn't his fault. Sometimes circumstances outside your control consume what little strength you have."

Dal smiled but it was a smile without mirth.

"Like your boyfriend?"

Kathy squirmed. "I suppose that's an example. It's true he's taken every reserve of strength I had."

"Then take it back."

"I can't. Unfortunately, he was even weaker than me. He used it all up."

Dal regarded her pensively, then stretched down to where her knapsack lay on the floor by her bed. She removed the wooden box with the Asian designs and extracted a vial of dark, green liquid.

"The Elixir of Inner Fortitude. This'll help you."

"Another vial?" Kathy frowned.

"You still doubt me?"

Although stung by the recrimination, Kathy was not in the mood to concede. "I don't think life's problems can be solved by a magic potion."

Dal shrugged.

"Magic's nothing more than an experience we don't fully understand. Essentially, it's just like science — a concept we use to try and make sense of something. The difference is that where science focuses on the reduction of doubt, magic lingers in that no-man's land where uncertainty ends and theoretical knowledge begins." She sniffed. "Think about it! A tribesman in Borneo would consider a television magical. Children consider everything magical, until we rush in to inform them there's a logical reason for it. I think it'd be a bit unwise to simply dismiss something just because it's described as magic."

She regarded Kathy closely.

"Besides, what do you have to lose?"

With that simple statement, Kathy knew that Dal had effectively struck the essence of her situation. She really had nothing to lose. Nothing.

"All right," she sighed. "I'll try it."

Dal nodded. Removing the tiny cork, she handed the vial to Kathy.

"What do I have to do?"

"Just drink."

Kathy raised the vial to her lips, swallowing the contents in a single gulp. The liquid was surprisingly light and tasteless — like drinking damp air.

"What happens next?"

Dal refilled their glasses.

"We toast one another."

They saluted each other solemnly and drained the contents.

Kathy licked her lips. "Have you ever tried one of your own potions?"

Dal chewed her lower lip. "Yes," she admitted at last. "Once. About two years ago. The day I received my father's hat."

Kathy regarded her with interest. "Which one did you take?"

"The Elixir of Unequivocal Forgiveness."

Kathy stared at her blankly.

"My father," said Dal. "He was … like your boyfriend. He used to beat my mother. One day he slapped her around too hard. When she was climbing to the trapeze rig before a performance in Belgium she slipped. Her arms couldn't take the strain and …"

She sniffed and rubbed her nose.

"I never lived with my father after that. He refused to accept responsibility for what he'd done. He insisted it was just an accident. Like I said, he was never really a strong man."

She replaced the vial in its box.

"Towards the end he finally acknowledged it. At least, I think that's why he sent me his hat. Among ringmasters, that's the equivalent of handing over your sword, of admitting defeat."

Dal turned away then and seemed to shrink inside herself. Kathy, numbly, continued to stare at her, struggling to absorb what she'd been told. Reaching for her glass, she made to pick it up but for some reason it slipped between her fingers and onto the floor. Confused, she felt herself falling too, sliding back against the wall until she was looking at the room from an awkward angle. For one precise moment, she wondered at the strangeness of it all, then the last shards of peace tinkled in the back of her mind.

And the world just folded itself away.

She slept the sleep of the dead. Her slumber was deep, insensible, more intense than any she could recall. She felt nothing, dreamed nothing, although at one time she was vaguely aware that it was raining.

She awoke in a haze of absolute clarity, of watery sunshine streaming through a gap in the curtains.

The mist had disappeared.

Rising from the bed, she found that although her mind was clear, her body was weak and dehydrated. She struggled to her feet, her head heavy and her muscles leaden with a flu-like ache.

She realised then that she was completely naked. Her blouse, skirt, even her underwear were gone. Wrapping herself in a sheet, she leaned wearily against the wall and looked around the room. There was no sign of Dal, although her clothes — the purple shirt, red jacket and pants — lay neatly folded by her knapsack at the end of her bed, topped by the ever-prominent top hat. Her gaze swung to the bare bedside table where she'd left her briefcase and wallet.

"Shit!"

She staggered to Dal's bed and rummaged through the knapsack, but it contained nothing more than an assortment of colourful clothing. Her actions disturbed the top hat and it toppled over, revealing her wallet and passport beneath. Inserted in her wallet she found a hand-written invoice for a 'spiritual consultation' that had apparently cost her clothing and a brief note that read:

I'm sorry, Kathy. Drowsiness was a side-effect I neglected to mention. Enjoy your new life.

Dal

Stripped of fog, the street outside the Dog's Bollox was unrecognizable. Although she had assumed it was flat and straight, it was, in fact, a gentle slope that curved down to the harbour, lined on either side by an irregular array of stone houses. The air was heavy with the scent of salt, and the sea was visible over the roofs of the nearest houses. In the distance she could see several boats and an island.

Leaving the B&B in Dal's clothing, she felt uncomfortably conspicuous in the colourful apparel and held the top hat in her hand, obscured as far as possible by the bulk of the knapsack.

She stumbled towards the railway station, her light-headedness adding a dreamlike quality to her passage and hindering her efforts to make sense of the previous night's events.

She was surprised by her own lack of reaction, the lack of any regret for her business suit or briefcase. If anything, their absence was strangely liberating.

At the station, Kathy passed through the central concourse, emerging outside on the station's single quay. Two trains were drawn up alongside the platforms on either side. The electronic departure boards indicated that one of them, destined for the city, was scheduled to leave in the next two minutes. The other, bound for Dover and the continental ferry terminal, was due to depart less than three minutes later.

A sense of repugnance washed over Kathy as she regarded the city train. Suddenly, her features softened and she started to laugh, a surprisingly beautiful and fragile laugh that gushed into the air until it was drowned out by the squeal of a departure whistle. A few seconds later the doors of the train slid shut with a soft automatic hum. Jolting gently into motion, it began to pull away from the station.

"Are you a magician?"

Kathy turned to find a little girl standing beside her, examining her costume with interest.

"What?"

"Are you a magician?" repeated the girl.

Kathy stared at the girl for several seconds. "Yes," she replied at last. "Do you believe in magic?"

"Oh yes," said the girl quite firmly.

"That's good." Leaning down, Kathy whispered into the girl's ear.

"Close your eyes and count to thirty. When you open them again I'll have disappeared."

The clouds tipped their caps and the first drops of rain began to fall. A shrill whistle pealed down the length of the platform and a stray raindrop splashed on her face, but the girl ignored it all as she slowly and meticulously counted to thirty.

Sex with Sarah

Every Friday evening Sarah arrives at my door to fuck for half an hour, sip peppermint tea and take a taxi home. Our relationship is what the French would call a *cinq à sept* — an office fling between those most critical of Gallic milestones, the termination of the workday and the commencement of dinner.

I never invite Sarah to prolong her visit. We have an agreement to respect each other's privacy, to maintain our distance by limiting our affection to the tit-bits of post-coital interaction. Sarah's unique ability in this respect is one of the many things that intrigue me about her. It fascinates me that she can take part in such unrestrained carnal activity, then thirty minutes and a short taxi ride later, slip effortlessly into a separate existence with all the ease of a foot sliding into a comfortable old shoe.

I lust after Sarah.

It is a basic fact of life. The reality of policies, however, that discourage fraternisation between Ministry staff and contractors like myself, ensures that our liaison remains discreet. Such blinkered disregard for the nature of sexual relationships is typical of the many little hypocrisies within the Wellington bureaucracy. In that cloistered mindset you will always find deluded individuals who believe in the moderating influence of corporate values. Deep down, however, deep beneath the layers of corporate gloss and political correctness, the spectre of lust retains the ability to drag us from our airy pedestals when we least expect it.

Given the smouldering potential between Sarah and I, it was inevitable that sex would impact on our professional relationship. So it was, that when we found ourselves alone in the aftermath of a Friday evening office celebration, all professional and corporate standards were willingly compromised. The sex that night was more vital than any I'd previously experienced, the final orgasm a liquescent explosion that reverberated through the hills of Wellington.

Five months on, although the venue has changed, Friday evenings remain a recurring appointment in our weekly schedules. At work we continue to treat each other with professional courtesy but beyond the restrictions of the office environment Friday evenings remain our regular weekly transgression.

Our dirty little secret.

I watch as Sarah's ribcage flutters from the tremors of her orgasm. Her body is svelte and supple, her stomach flat from regular sessions at the gym. Her shoulder-length black hair is professionally styled. When she smiles, she reveals a bright curve of perfect teeth framed by a pair of full red lips.

That evening those teeth draw blood, biting into my shoulder at the height of a culminating shudder. Afterwards she grins apologetically, then dabs the wound with antiseptic. Pulling a cigarette packet from her gym-bag, she slips back beneath the duvet and we lie in silence watching the smoke twist up to the ceiling.

"What's wrong?" I ask at last.

Her eyes remain closed, and for a moment I think she's sleeping.

"Sorry, I was thinking about the project."

"Ah."

I say nothing more but it's too late to prevent the twinge of conscience. Contracted by the Ministry to carry out an independent review of several internal projects, my investigation of an operational pilot for which Sarah is responsible has revealed some significant flaws in the initial design. One of the favoured candidates for a vacant general-manager position, Sarah is understandably concerned about the potential impact of my final report.

I have to confess I have no corporate career ambitions. Sarah, conversely, is a shining example of a career civil servant. An exemplary bureaucrat for the new millennium, she is a tireless workaholic, performing her professional activities with the same intensity as her sexual activities. Innovative and enthusiastic, she's regularly cited by the chief executive as the gold standard to which other managers should aspire, the yardstick against which all other women can measure their success and failure.

Despite her vigour and enthusiasm, however, Sarah's ambition is tainted with an unsettling sense of urgency, a kind of muted desperation aggravated by the recent celebration of her 35th birthday. That particular event has somehow undermined her confidence and made her fearfully aware of passing time. It has also increased her desire for challenge, to prove herself the equal and superior to her peers.

As the sun slides behind the Wadestown hills, the splinters of sunlight grow wan and fade. In the deepening gloom I can sense the silence lodge between us, growing fat on my discomfort and coldly sucking the moment dry.

When Sarah leaves I sit on the deck to absorb the panoramic huddle of Wellington harbour. In a rare and most uncharacteristic act of restraint, the wind, that most essential feature of Wellington life, has eased to a soundless hush and receded out of existence. Down on the harbour the water has the alien smoothness of unblemished glass.

The absence of wind smothers the city with a heavy calm that muffles the urban bustle. A solitary vehicle putters on the Wadestown Road, a mother calls her child to dinner. A dog barks twice then stops as silence gushes in to fill the void. Only the noise of the cicadas penetrates the stifled atmosphere, floating up from the surrounding vegetation like the crackle of static.

I wince as I examine the wound on my shoulder, irritated that once again I've come off the worse in our coupling.

Over the past few weeks a subtle change has infiltrated our Friday evenings, displacing the pleasure with a gruelling physical exercise that's fleetingly rewarding but ultimately debilitating. The sex feels wrong, tastes wrong and despite my efforts I'm unable to recapture the simplicity of our original couplings. Where it should leave us polished, it leaves us worn and ragged. Where it should leave us renewed, it leaves us shabby and frayed.

Sometimes, when I sprawl hollow-eyed and gasping from another explosive encounter, Sarah continues to masturbate beside me, fucking herself into deep ecstatic oblivion. As I lie there, spent and prostrate, I wonder if that is what she seeks from sex: the opportunity to obliterate herself, to lose all perception of thought and self in those drawn-out, screaming orgasms.

"Sarah," says Cass. "She never stays the night."

"She has other obligations."

"Ah."

My flatmate Cassandra smiles, but it's clearly an effort. The heartless slopes of Wellington have been particularly hard on her today and her cycle-courier uniform is soiled with sweat. She runs a hand through her spiked blonde hair and raises a glass of wine as she drinks in the view. Shifting her balance from one foot to the other, she flexes the muscles in her calves with the unconscious ease of a natural athlete.

I've grown to love this little Friday night ritual of wine and weed on the deck of the house we rent in Wadestown. Here we sip and talk the week away, watching the shades of mauve on the Orongorongo hills slowly lose their grip in the dying sunlight and slip down to the harbour waters.

Cass puffs on the joint and releases a perfect ring of smoke. It hangs in the stillness of the night like some kind of prophetic omen before it finally dissipates.

"Not bad."

She grins and passes the joint to me.

"Four-more-weeks." She utters each word slowly. Deliberately.

"Until?"

"Until I finish my exams. Then I can apply for a real job, become a public servant."

I think about that over a mouthful of wine, struggling to picture this athletic free spirit in the stifling confines of a government office.

"Why would you want to work in the civil service, Cass?"

"To help people, I suppose. You might think it's corny but I'd like to think I could have some input into making this country a better place. And I'd like to do it well. Maybe, one day, even as well as Sarah."

"Sarah!"

"As a civil service role model you'd have to admit she's one of the best."

"Mmm," I answer vaguely.

Cass's ongoing professional infatuation with Sarah continues to surprise me, long after I've accepted that it's hardly unusual. In the peculiar position of professional 'pin-up' girl for the civil service, she is often promoted as a role model for students of public policy like Cassandra.

"Cass, I should warn you about unrealistic expectations. Helping people is probably the last thing you'd be doing as a civil servant."

"What do you mean?"

I swallow a mouthful of red wine.

"Well, the truth is civil servants work within the confines of a great bureaucratic paradigm. They're obliged to use a distinct vocabulary, follow specific channels and observe codes of conduct that some would consider unreasonably restrictive. Most importantly, they also have to adhere to a service mindset dictated by politicians."

"So?"

"So most of the policy analysis carried out by officials automatically places the good of the Government before the good of the public. One could argue that the country's national decision making processes are fundamentally tainted because they're based on political and financial dictates as opposed to social or moral criteria."

"Rubbish," laughs Cass. "I have several friends in the civil service who enjoy helping people."

"Sure. But they're mostly at the lower end of the corporate ladder — which is fine if they're happy to remain there. If you have aspirations to rise in the ranks, however, you'll find that the higher you climb the more pressure is applied to adhere to political expectations. The sad truth is that you sometimes have to accept political realities to achieve a desired goal."

I shrug.

"Needless to say, the long-term effect of compromising one's ethical values is the gradual erosion of your personal integrity. That's why, in general, it's unwise to trust a career bureaucrat."

Cass tilts her glass to capture the last red dregs of liquid sunbeams.

"I'll never allow that to happen to me."

"Of course you won't."

She twists her lips thoughtfully.

"Was that why you left?"

I smile, genuinely impressed. "Something like that. I suppose you could say I didn't like the person I was becoming."

I offer her the joint but she shakes her head.

"Are you ever going to introduce me to Sarah? I'd really like to meet her in person."

"No. Get some friends your own age."

Her sudden laugh startles us both. It resonates through the night, tumbling down the bush-coated slope to Thorndon like thunder from an incoming storm. She leans against the railing and considers the harbour.

"Our lecturer says that establishing contacts early in one's career is essential for budding bureaucrats."

"I'm sure you'll flower just as well by yourself."

"So you're not going to help."

"I am helping. I'm ensuring you have the strength of character to do the right thing at the right time."

"Ah!" Her mouth turns up in a cynical smile. "Such integrity! Is that why Sarah likes you?"

"No. Sarah likes me because I give her something she needs."

Sensing a rare admission, Cass leans forwards with conspiratorial interest. "Romance?" she suggests. "Love?"

I shake my head and stub the joint in an ash-filled paua shell.

"Relief."

The heavy cloud of silence continues to smother the city throughout the weekend. By Monday afternoon, Wellingtonians accustomed to the background murmur of wind have grown appreciably twitchy. They start at the slightest flutter of air, the merest draught rustling through the streets like a silent rumour. I can't help but notice the way their eyes veer off in the middle of a conversation, scanning the hills and harbour for squall shadow or flecks of foam.

Cass calls me at work later that afternoon and asks if I can meet her. Surprised, I leave the office and walk to Midland Park, where I find her sitting by the fountain with a takeaway coffee in each hand.

"Don't look now," she says as I take a seat beside her, "but someone by the taxi stand seems to be taking an unusual interest in you."

I glance towards the taxi stand, immediately recognizing the grey-haired man in a suit who's watching us both intently. He smiles as my eyes fall on him, waves amiably, then slowly turns to cross the street.

"Who was that?" asks Cass, genuinely intrigued.

"Anthony Hamilton. Chief executive at the Ministry."

Cass observes the departing figure.

"Does he live in Oriental Bay?"

"Yes."

"Aaah," she nods. "I thought I recognised the name. I've delivered several packages to his house over the last few weeks."

"Evidently nothing escapes the scrutiny of the vigilant courier network."

Cass laughs easily, popping the cover of her coffee.

"We don't miss much. You get to cycling around this city so often that after a while you can feel its pulse through the handlebars."

She hands me the second coffee.

"Why did you want to see me, Cass?"

She fidgets with the strap of her helmet.

"There's an advertisement in Saturday's paper for analysts in Sarah's department. They're looking for new graduates and ..."

"And you've decided to apply."

"Yeeeees," she admits. "I was hoping you'd be willing to act as a referee."

I close my eyes, savouring the raw taste of liquid caffeine on the back of my tongue. For just one brief moment I focus on that sensation, then open my eyes and put the coffee aside.

"Before I can answer that there's something I need to show you. Have you got time for a stroll?"

Cass considers me curiously but nods and rises to get her bicycle. She wheels it alongside as I lead her away from the park and down Featherston Street towards the Central Library. We ascend the walkway up to the City to Sea Bridge and halt at a spot overlooking the City Council crèche. The sound of children's laughter ripples up around us like a skittish cloud of butterflies.

"Well?" asks Cass. "Why did you drag me all the way down here?"

"See those two little girls?" I gesture down at the crèche, indicating a pair of dark-haired girls in red frocks playing by an empty tractor tyre. "What age would you put the eldest at?"

Cass shrugs. "I dunno. About five?"

"Close. She's four years old. The other girl's about two."

Cass regards me warily. "What's all this about?"

"They're Sarah's kids."

Cass looks at me blankly for several seconds, then slowly turns to stare at the girls. As we watch, the younger one stumbles, scratching her knee on a piece of concrete. The older girl reaches over to hug her as she starts to cry, comforting her until a caregiver arrives.

Cass doesn't say anything for several moments. "What are you trying to tell me?" she asks at last.

"I'm not trying to tell you anything. I'm just showing you Sarah's daughters."

"I ... I didn't know she had ..."

"I know. Sarah retains her maiden name for career purposes but she's married, Cass. Her relationship with me is nothing more than an extra-marital affair. There's intimacy and genuine affection but there's no sharing and the big 'L' certainly doesn't enter the equation. To be honest, it's so physical it's almost superficial."

Cass stares at the ground, repeatedly stubbing the toe of her shoe against the wall.

"Why are you doing this?"

"I don't want you to have any illusions about me. Or Sarah."

Cass glares at me. "This is all part of having the strength of character to do the right thing, is it?"

There's no real answer to that so I remain silent.

Cass spins abruptly, wheeling her bike back in towards Lambton Quay. As I watch her walk I hear the children's laughter again and become aware of a breeze brushing my face.

The Wellington winds have finally returned.

―――

When I return to the Ministry that afternoon, Sarah's standing by the window in my office, flicking through the draft report on her project.

"Ah, you're back!" She drops the document onto the table. "I wanted to thank you for letting me see this." She pokes it gently with the tip of her fingernail. "Has anybody else seen it yet?"

"No. I shouldn't even have let you look at it."

"Mmm," she nods, and thinks about that for a moment. "Look, I really need to know. Are you absolutely sure there's no way of improving the conclusions?"

"I'm sorry, Sarah. I can't change the results."

"Of course not!" She pauses. "But you could report them in a different manner."

I gaze through the window. In a neighbouring building a man in a business suit is working in an office almost identical to my own, typing feverishly on a laptop with tight, jerky movements.

I slowly turn back to Sarah. She has the decency to blush.

"I'm sorry. Forget I even said that."

She shuffles a pile of papers on my desk, fumbles, then spills them to the floor. Bending down, she replaces them on the desk, coughs quietly and clears her throat.

"When do you submit the final report?"

"In two weeks. On my last day with the Ministry."

"Oh!" says Sarah. "Your last day."

There's a long silence.
"Sarah, where are we going with this?"
"With what?"
"With us! Do we stop seeing one another once I've left the Ministry? Should we stop Friday evenings?"

This time it's Sarah who turns to stare through the window, oblivious to the reflection looking back at her. I place a hand on her shoulder.

"Sarah, we're not going to resolve this until we talk it over."

She surprises me by taking my hand in hers — a remarkably affectionate gesture for Sarah. "Sometimes," she says sadly, "that's the point."

Cassandra avoids me for the remainder of the week, carrying herself with a wounded nobility that makes me want to curl up inside. It's an understandable reaction to the callous manner in which I'd thrashed her career aspirations, predominantly out of a need to mollify my own guilt. When I finally corner her in the lounge to apologise she responds with an honest simplicity that makes me feel even worse.

"I can't really resent you for telling the truth," she says. "I was naive. I'll get over it."

She retires to her room and I remain alone to watch the sun slide behind the hills in shame.

The wind grows steadily over the following week. By Friday, gales hurtle wildly overhead and the city is hunkered deep into the green nooks and crannies of the Wellington topography.

When I answer the door for Sarah that evening, I notice that the fallen Pohutukawa stamens coating my doorstep like a tattered red carpet for over a week have finally been blown away.

Throwing her gym-bag in its usual spot, she starts to undress in the lounge. I catch a glimpse of the little white stretch marks on her stomach — those physical scars of childbirth that always remind me of ladders in a woman's tights.

"Sarah," I ask her. "What's it like having children?"

Sarah stares at me in astonishment. We've never broached the topic of her family before.

"It makes you grown up," she says at last. "And less selfish."

"Because …?"

"Because you have to care for someone else apart from yourself. It's like being on call. For 24 hours of the day."

"It sounds like a pain."

"It is. But it's also a pleasure."

"Like sex?" I tease.

She shakes her head. "Nothing like sex. Sex is a selfish act, an egocentric indulgence that I justify by telling myself it keeps me sane. Through our Friday evenings together I prove to myself that I'm an individual with my own life — not just a parent in a family unit or a stereotypical career woman. It's also self-centred in that I'm being unfaithful to my husband and negligent of my children."

"I don't understand. So how does having children make you less selfish?"

Her smile is sad.

"Because it makes me feel guilty about it."

Such talk seems to ignite something inside her, for the next thing I know we're clawing at each other, tugging at each other as we tumble to the lounge floor. There on the hardwood surface we empty all thought in a senseless physical rush, screwing and screwing until there's nothing left to fill, nothing left to release, and nothing to burn but friction. Although I come, my ejaculation lacks any exultance. It is nothing more than a mechanical, perfunctory emptying. Like someone else's discharge.

When we pull apart, shell-shocked and dazed by the viciousness of our coupling, I discover that my body is covered with marks; deep scratches along my back and shoulders, teeth marks on my neck. Blue bruises blossom along the inside of Sarah's thighs.

Forgoing her shower and peppermint tea, Sarah dresses quietly in her gym gear and slips through the door without saying goodbye. I watch wordlessly as she leaves, too exhausted to call after her.

The weather is too severe to occupy my habitual seat on the deck but tonight that suits my mood. Tonight I have a great craving for darkness and silence, an instinctive need to retreat deep inside myself.

Exhausted, I collapse onto the sofa, to find Sarah's suit and starched white shirt lying forgotten on the sidearm. Her scent fills my nostrils as I sleep.

That night I dream of two little girls in pohutukawa frocks.

Over my final week at the Ministry I immerse myself in my work, focusing solely on the completion of my reports, and withdrawing from social interaction with staff. I see little of Sarah over these final days and our few brief encounters are noteworthy only for their awkwardness.

I have a growing sense of falling away from Sarah, but my despair is tinged with a conflicting sense of relief. I realise that by raising the subject of her family prior to sex I've disrupted the romantic illusion that disguises the true nature of every adulterous affair and forced us to confront our selfishness.

Back home, although the frostiness of my relationship with Cassandra has thawed, our conversations remain stilted. In the evenings, to avoid the effort of communication, I take to walking by the waterfront. There I search for calm in empty spaces between the waves thrown up by the rising wind.

On Friday afternoon I submit the final reports to Anthony Hamilton and he accepts them graciously. He also presses me to attend a function that evening to celebrate his successful seven-year run as chief executive. Tired and subdued, I am persuaded only by the realisation that Sarah is organising it and that there won't be another opportunity to talk with her before leaving the Ministry.

After a long shower and a change of clothes, I return to a party that appears to take up the entire first floor of the Ministry building. As government department functions go, Anthony's is a surprisingly bright affair with live music from a quartet of classical musicians, and a large number of senior officials and politicians. Anthony dominates the proceedings with his characteristic authority, occupying a raised area in the centre of the room while his wife, an elegant woman with a pretty face, smiles happily by his side.

Lacking any real desire for social interaction, I sip some wine in a quiet corner and scan the crowd for Sarah. Individual snippets of conversation brush my ears and I wince at the incessant references to Ministers and policy objectives, experiencing a familiar repugnance for the wearying hypocrisy of political correctness in which I've, once again, become ensnared.

A gentle tap on the shoulder drags me away from this melancholy train of thought and I turn to the attractive female figure standing by me.

"Cass!"

I'm dumbfounded, stunned not only by her unexpected presence but also that she's wearing Sarah's suit.

Cass grasps my hand. Her eyes are soft.

"We need to talk," she says.

Sarah's familiar scent alerts me to her presence even before her lips brush my ear. Her eyes follow my line of sight to where Cass is nervously chatting with two smooth young officials vying for her attention.

"Who's that?" she whispers.

"My flatmate."

She appraises Cass for several seconds. "Young," she decides at last. "But pretty." She makes to turn away, then stops and stares at Cass again. "Christ! She's wearing my clothes!"

I smile dryly.

"I'm afraid so. She wanted to see me but needed a suit to get past security and into the building. She didn't have any so she borrowed yours."

I expect Sarah to get angry but she surprises me by nodding in approval.

"Tell her to keep it. It suits her. Besides, I've got several others."

She taps the side of her glass with smooth red fingernails. "Have you submitted the final reports?"

"Yes. This afternoon." I withdraw a stapled document from my jacket pocket and hand it to her. "I thought you might appreciate a copy."

Sarah accepts the document, smiling gratefully as she flips to the 'Conclusions'. She scans it then stops, slowly raising her head to consider me with a tight smile.

"You haven't changed it."

"Did you think I would?"

She shuffles uncomfortably.

"No, but I was hoping you might."

I look across the room to where Anthony is having a preliminary glance at some notes for his speech, then turn back to Sarah. Standing there in the soft glow of an artificial chandelier, her face looks more angular, the features tighter than I've ever noticed before. She stares at me. I stare at her. We do not touch.

"You know!"

Her voice is tight, a strangled mumble expelled on a gasp of air.

"I know."

I swallow my wine and place the empty glass on a nearby table.

"I found out a few minutes ago." I gesture vaguely in Cass's direction. "My flatmate's a courier. You'd be surprised what couriers see. Apparently, they don't miss much. Take this morning, for example. When she was dropping off a package she saw a friend of mine in her underwear through the window of Anthony's mansion."

Sarah seems to fold in on herself, shrinking into the ensuing silence.

"I'll assume you have the GM post sewn up, then?"

"I'm sorry! Jesus, I'm so sorry!"

"Please," I say. "Let's not do this."

Anthony stands to commence his speech and the room bursts into applause.

Sometimes it's best to simply walk away — not to turn the other cheek so much as move it out of range.

As we walk away from the Ministry that night, Cass's face is pale in the frostbitten moonlight and a single tear slides down one glacial cheekbone.

"Bastards!" she says.

I put an arm around her, grateful for the distraction from the emptiness that eats me up inside. I understand the irony of Cass's disenchantment even as I understand that I really have no right to feel betrayal. In the precarious existence of the Wellington bureaucracy, Sarah has lost her grip on everything that's important, trampling her own humanity as she's driven onwards by the whiplash of her own ambition. In an environment where success is measured by job titles and political survival, no one could dispute that Sarah will excel.

A taxi drops us back to the house where we immediately light up a joint on the deck and open a bottle of wine to toast the glimmering city below. In minutes we've slipped back into the comforting intimacy of our routine but even as I commence the overdose of wine and heady fumes I know that this is nothing but a temporary respite. Deep into the twilight hours I'll resurface in the silence, mourning after Sarah. As the shadows fade from the incoming dawn, I'll watch the shades of mauve on the Orongorongo hills slowly lose their grip and slip down to the harbour waters.

Until the wind has blown our sins away.

And I can, at long last, sleep.

The morning after

I DISCOVERED THE NAKED BODY on the corner of the bed, lodged between the headboard and the largest pillow. A brunette in her fifties, I stared at her in bleary-eyed fascination despite the heavy pounding behind my temple.

Ah Jaysus! I thought. What have you gone and done now!

I managed to roll onto one side, although it was something of an effort. My body ached all over and a gut-clenching nausea required a conscious effort on my part to prevent it from spilling up into something altogether more tangible. I hacked up a fur ball of phlegm, cigarette smoke and unidentifiable particulate matter, wincing at the tremors of pain it produced. Evidently I'd surpassed all previous scales of excess and was probably eligible for the *Guinness Book of Records* on the state of my intestines alone.

Grunting, I sat up to examine my surroundings — a large, expensively furnished room that was completely unfamiliar.

My coughing had roused the woman beside me. Groaning, she raised one creased eyelid to reveal a bloodshot, unfocused orb beneath. She was quite skinny with a face that would have been beautiful once but had long since been gnarled by age and temperament.

"Uuuuh. Who are you?" she moaned in a nasal American twang.

A fair question, albeit one I found myself, bizarrely, unable to answer. I'd absolutely no idea who I was or how I'd ended up in bed with her.

"I don't know," I croaked from a throat that sounded as though it had smoked a thousand cigarettes. "Who are you?"

Threads of dried saliva stretched from her lips as she attempted to speak.

"Barbara."

"Barbara who?"

She shook her head, then winced. "I don't remember."

I wondered momentarily at the coincidence of our shared amnesia, then shrugged gamely. "Ah, sure, Barbara is a lovely name!"

Somehow through the hangover she managed to give me a look of withering contempt — no small feat given the obvious effort it required. After a moment or two, however, the expression faded, melding into one of confusion, then subsequent panic as her complete lack of clothing registered.

Aghast, she sprang up with an enthusiasm that was not shared by her body. Before she'd even reached the upright position, the hangover kicked in and she fell back onto the bed, writhing in pain.

It took her a minute or two to summon the strength to try again. This time, avoiding any sudden movements, she cautiously wrapped herself in the bedsheet before sitting up. From the look on her face it was obvious that she, too, was unfamiliar with our present location. Returning her attention to me, she shuddered involuntarily as her eyes absorbed my pot-belly and receding hairline.

"Did we, ah ..." she left the sentence unfinished but the look of horror on her face said it all.

"Well, if we didn't ..." I said with some malice "... some dirty pervert has smeared marmalade all over my genitals and painted me arse with lipstick!"

"Oh, sweet Lord!"

Overwhelmed by some violent inner vision, she recoiled backwards off the bed. There was a crunching sound as she hit the floor and, crawling hastily to the edge, I gawped down to where she was lying dazed in a discordant jumble of potato chips, wine bottles, porn mags, vibrators, and the soiled remnants of what looked suspiciously like a shredded Supergirl costume.

"Are you all right?"

A panic-stricken expression swept over her face as she absorbed the nature of her resting place. She practically levitated from the floor in her desperation to expunge a particularly adhesive condom.

"Get it off me! Oh my God, you filthy animal!"

Clambering from the bed, I moved to help her up but she slapped my hands away.

"Get away from me, you pervert!"

Pulling herself off the floor, she staggered against the wall and wiped off all remaining detritus. "Could you please …" she hissed "… cover yourself!"

She continued to glower as I wrapped myself in another bedsheet until some unexpected thought appeared to flit across her features. Her eyes bulged and her brow creased up in surprise. "Sweet Jesus!" she said with obvious consternation. "My bottom hurts."

Sheepishly, I stared at the ground and said nothing.

We were both equally keen to depart the scene of our depravity. Stumbling through the bedroom door, we found ourselves in a bright hallway that stretched for several metres before curving sharply into another room. Sunlight tumbled down warmly through a series of skylights, falling softly onto a collection of pornographic photographs that lined the walls on either side.

Bloody hell, I thought to myself. Where the hell are we?

Barbara peered at the nearest photo, blinked, and snarled. "What am I doing here? Among all this … degeneracy! I'm a good woman! I know I am. I shouldn't be here!"

"Ah, sure, of course you are. I'm sure its all some terrible mistake."

I considered her from the corner of my eye, still struggling to imagine how I could have possibly have ended up in carnal relations with such a cantankerous old trout. "Do you remember anything at all?" I asked.

She surveyed me sullenly.

"I remember Rome," she said at last.

"Rome!"

"I think I was there …" she hesitated, "… for the confirmation of the new Pope."

"Hang on!" I exclaimed. "I'm sure I was there too."

And it was true. I remembered a large crowd, an event of great ceremony at the Vatican and, afterwards, some kind of formal celebration with food and drink.

There'd been a lot of drink.

After that, however, things turned decidedly hazy. I had a vague memory of a nightclub with lots of well dressed people, then another, seedier nightclub, but after that things got particularly murky and all I recalled were individual snippets of more drink, joints, and large numbers of coloured pills.

The hallway led into a broad living area where one wall, almost entirely glass, looked down over a busy inner-city district. We were, I realized, in the upper levels of some up-town apartment block.

"My god!" Barbara pointed to a dark structure, silhouetted against the pale, afternoon skyline. "The Eiffel Tower! We're not even in Rome. This is Paris."

I stared in horror. How in god's name had we ended up in Paris?

I had a sudden, mind-wrenching recollection. Hadn't there been a plane? Someone's private jet, full of party-goers engaged in a raucous singsong? There'd certainly been an airhostess dressed in red, passing a tray of drinks around.

Actually, no. Come to think of it, that'd been a transvestite holding a mirror with several lines of white powder.

While I was struggling to make sense of my mangled memories, the shock of finding herself in another country apparently proved all too much for Barbara. Lurching from the lounge, she stumbled into a nearby bathroom and seconds later the painful sound of retching echoed through the open doorway.

Once the noise subsided I entered the bathroom to find her sitting on the floor by the toilet bowl, regarding the extent of her oral destruction with vague stupefaction.

"Are you all right?"

"I've just had an epiphany!" she declared.

"Oh?"

She wiped the back of her hand across her chin. "When I was looking down into the bowl, I saw a face staring back up at me. It was a man's face. A familiar face." She paused. "I think I'm married."

"Ah, that's lovely news," I exclaimed. "Congratulations!"

We found some paracetamol in a kitchenette and swallowed a number of capsules with glasses of cool, untainted water. Several envelopes addressed to a 'Monsieur Fredo' were strewn around the bench. The name meant nothing to either of us but, I suspected, had some connection to the swarthy individual with the gold medallion who graced several large photographs adorning the walls.

Barbara thoughtfully regarded one of the photographs. "I remember that face," she grimaced. "He gave me a glass of wine at the ceremony. The satyr! He probably put a drug in my drink."

Further exploration revealed another bedroom with a large walk-in wardrobe that contained an assortment of clothing, predominantly suits and garish silk shirts. Sorting through the various items, we eventually found some that fitted approximately and regarded our reflections sombrely in the bedroom mirror. "We look like a pair of pimps!"

"Somehow," said Barbara, "that seems remarkably apt."

I studied her reflection closely.

"You know, you look awfully familiar. Have we met before?"

"Please!" She grimaced again.

"I'm serious. I'm sure I recognise your face from somewhere."

"Hah!"

"Aaaah, come on, Barbara."

She glared at me.

"I'm going to have you incarcerated, you know. You do realise that, don't you? I'll going to have you locked away so long they'll throw away the key!"

Casting one last poisonous glance in my direction, she turned on her heel and stormed from the room.

"Ah, Jaysus!" I exclaimed.

Disturbed by Barbara's unrestrained hostility, I flopped onto the side of the bed and sighed. Pulling a magazine from the bedside cabinet, I half-heartedly flicked through it as I considered her threat. I was about to toss the magazine aside when a colourful photo on the cover caught my eye. I gaped incredulously for several seconds then, heart pounding, flicked to the contents page and on to a number of articles and other photographs in the centre pages.

"Well, bugger me!" I thought.

It took several minutes before I felt sufficiently composed to return to the main room. When I got there I found Barbara shouting furiously into the mouthpiece of the telephone.

"Police! P, O, fucking L, I, C, E! Police! Christ! Can't you morons speak English!!"

"Barbara."

"What?"

I held up the magazine. "You need to see this."

"I think I've seen about as much of you as I can stomach."

"No, really."

She turned slowly to face me, mouth opening to release a fresh stream of invective when her eyes locked onto the magazine I was holding like a shield before me. Her jaw dropped when she saw her face on the cover, superimposed against an image of the American flag. Beside her, looking adoringly into her eyes, was the president of the United States.

"Oh, Christ!" said Barbara.

Oddly enough, Barbara wasn't too pleased to learn that she was the First Lady of the United States. As she flipped through the magazine it was obvious that the memories were flooding back, but judging from the deepening frown on her face, the revelations only served to dismay her further.

I tried to offer her a nice cup of tea, but she didn't appear in the mood to appreciate it.

"It'll do you good," I insisted.

She sniffed disdainfully.

"Ah come on, Barbara! Sure, it could be an awful lot worse."

Her eyes burned with undisguised contempt.

"Really!" she snarled and the venom in her voice seared the air between us. "Let's just recap on that for a second, shall we? I'm married to the president of the United States, I have two children, I'm a God-fearing Christian and yet, for some bizarre reason I cannot even start to comprehend, I've somehow managed to betray my husband, my religion, my country — not to mention my own standards of decency — by engaging in sex with an ugly, lecherous, Irish Lothario." She paused and breathed deeply before continuing.

"How could it possibly be any worse?"

Irritably, I reached for the magazine and flipped to the centre page. "Well, Barbara," I said as I held it up for her to see. "It could be worse, because it turns out I'm the new Pope!"

Fridge

I MURDERED MY FRIDGE one night. A dagger deep in its entrails. It never stood a chance.

Actually, it was a steak knife embedded in the gas tube, but what the hell! For weeks afterwards my wife insists on telling me that you should never attempt to clean the icebox of the freezer with a knife when the fridge is defrosting. "Let it melt!" she says. "Let it melt. It'll take a bit of time but it'll melt."

"You should never try to clean the ice out with a knife!" For weeks. That's great! Thanks a lot! Why doesn't anybody ever share this gem of public information before one actually performs the deed? Humankind has a right to know. Now I have a dead fridge on my hands, a solid cubular body sitting motionless by the wall beneath the window.

Great.

Bloody marvellous!

When I murdered the fridge, the knife cut deep into the gas tube. Actually, it wasn't murder, it was manslaughter. I never intended to kill it. I had no motive, no profit gained. All I've got is sour milk and strange colours forming on the cheese.

I was trying to help it. Christ! Its lungs were all clogged up with big chunks of crystallised diamond water and frosty flakes of sugar powder. Poor sod was a goner anyway. Just tried to help. Knife slipped on a frictionless piece of ice. Stabbed the gas pipe. SSSSSSSSSSSSSSSSS!! Escaping gas. Bloody fridge hissin' at me like a snake. Sound dyin' out to a weak whisper as I edge my ear closer to hear its final words.

You know. Like in the movies where they say 'Tell Mom I love her' or something like that.

"You edged closer!" says my wife. "You edged closer! The pipes are full of freon gas. Freon gas is poisonous!" She tells me this for weeks afterwards. Weeks. Thanks. Bloody marvellous! Why the hell don't people let you in on this piece of information before you do the deed? Why do people hide these essential facts of life from the ones who actually need them?

Anyway. The fridge is dyin'. Try to hear what it says but it sounds like a rejected fart in my ear. Farting in my ear? Well thanks a lot, pal! Last time I try to help you! Last time anyone tries to help you, I guess.

I've got to get rid of the body. "Get rid of that body," my wife tells me. For weeks. Weeks! Have you ever tried lifting a dead fridge? They're bloody heavy, I can tell you!

Finally, I get around to hiring a car and a trailer for a few hours. All I have to do now is carry the body downstairs to the ground floor and drop it in the trailer. Then I'll wrap it in chains and dump it into a deep section of the river. I plan to wrap a carpet round the body, for two reasons.

One: That's the way it's always done in the movies. God knows why! If I passed someone lugging a carpet-wrapped object down the stairwell, the first thing I'd ask myself is where the hell is that guy going with the dead body? Perhaps its got something to do with grip.

Two: I can't remember the second reason.

Anyway. So there I am, fridge wrapped in a carpet, trying to lift it to the door of the stairwell. I'm heavin' and huffin' and puffin' out curses and gruntin' and kickin' the bloody fridge for being so heavy. That's when I try to raise it and, tryin' to get it onto the railing, I slip a disc in my back. Christ! That hurt like the devil himself was stabbin' me in the back.

"You tried to lift the fridge by yourself?" screams my wife. "You tried to lift the fridge by yourself? Are you crazy? That fridge weighs a ton!

Lifting weights does your back in! You'll never be able to raise weights again. Why didn't you call me for help?"

Her friends and my friends agree with her. "Why didn't you call us for help?" they ask me. My wife goes on for weeks afterwards. Weeks! Why the hell doesn't anyone offer to help until the deed is done? Here I am, stumblin' around my home like bleedin' Quasimodo on acid, fridgeless, out of milk, and I have to pay for the damage the fridge body caused when it fell off the bloody railing and plummeted through the floor and into the cellar.

Great!

Bloody marvellous!

For weeks my wife gives me hell about the carpet and the fridge and the railing and the hole in the floor and the damaged cellar and the bloody milk and the bloody cheese. Weeks! "What have you done to my carpet?" she asks me. "My priceless Turkish carpet. Why can't we have fresh milk?"

I murdered my wife last night.

Foreign correspondent

Maggie got the first card in November, deep in the glacial heart of a London winter. It was in her mailbox when she returned from work on a Friday evening and after yet another week of cheerlessly dark mornings, crypt-like evenings, and the daily commute through rain-drenched streets, the pale yellow envelope and bright French postage stamps appeared particularly incongruous. Surprised, she considered the envelope in the dim light of the foyer, glancing briefly at the address but failing to recognise the handwriting.

Struggling with the envelope, her briefcase and umbrella, she unlocked the door of her apartment and stepped inside. Her flat was a gloomy place, grey and cold, illuminated by a flickering neon sign outside the window that made it appear even colder. Kicking her boots off, she folded into a small sofa and opened the envelope to find a single postcard that had a print of Merten's 'Young Girl' on one side and a handwritten note on the other:

> Dear Ms Murphy
>
> Despite the years, thoughts of you continue to linger. I can still recall those long black curls, your penchant for woollen scarves and cowboy boots. Even now I can even hear the musical tones of your Irish accent. Sometimes I find you wandering through my mind, hands in your pockets as you kick a tin can around in my head.
>
> I have not forgotten.

There was nothing else. No signature, no return address, no indication who had sent it or why it had been addressed to her.

She remained sitting in the gloom of her living room for several minutes wondering why anyone would send such a strange card, particularly from overseas. She'd travelled extensively in her twenties but she'd never spent much time in France and couldn't think of anyone she knew who lived there.

She put the card and the envelope aside and stared out at the bleakness of another winter night. The darkness felt too comfortable to make the effort to rise to turn the lights on and she was too tired to bother cooking dinner. Retreating to her bedroom she crawled fully clothed beneath the duvet and fell asleep to the sound of hailstones commencing a fresh fusillade against the windowpanes.

She received her second piece of correspondence two weeks later. Returning home on a Friday evening she found another pale yellow envelope lying in her letterbox. As usual, the apartment was cold and uninviting. She sat in the sofa to open the letter and this time found a card with a picture of a naked woman set against a dark background. She read:

> Dear Ms Murphy
>
> I'd like to congratulate you on your recent promotion. I'm sure you must deserve it. I came across your photograph in a business magazine last week and learned that you were now a senior manager with Vitacomco. You look so professional in that picture, standing there in a tight black suit, starched white shirt and silver earrings. A true corporate warrior!
>
> I notice that you tie your hair up these days and I hope you don't mind me saying so, but it doesn't really suit you. It makes you look stiff and middle-aged and you're not even thirty-three by my calculations. Release those long black curls. Let them bounce on your shoulders like you used to. Then again, perhaps like me, you're starting to feel your age. Yes! Maybe that's it! You fear that your golden days too will fade away.
>
> Sincerely yours

Again, the note finished without any signature or return address. She rummaged through her papers until she found the original card and compared it with the latest. Both cards bore the same neat handwriting, and on the envelopes the addresses had been precisely written in the centre with the stamps placed perfectly on the top right-hand corner. Both were postmarked Lille, a city which she knew to be located in the north of France.

The cards offered no additional clues that she could decipher, so after a moment she laid them aside and put them from her mind. In the kitchen she heated up a microwave dinner from the freezer and took it to the breakfast bar. As she ate she watched an old Bogart movie on television about a grim detective smitten by his mysterious female client. Enthralled, she watched until the credits rolled and when the black and white screen was replaced by garish ads she switched it off and retired to bed.

The third envelope arrived a week later, another Friday in December. This time, however, she entered the foyer in a flurry of raindrops and jangling keys and grabbed the envelope from the post-box without glancing at it. The flat was its usual monotone dullness except for a small red light blinking on the display of her answering machine. Dropping everything onto the sofa, she hurried to the machine and pressed 'play.'

"Hi Maggie! It's Ben here. Sorry I didn't make it tonight but I had another appointment. I tried calling but couldn't remember your work number. Not to worry, eh. We can do dinner another night. I'll give you a call. See ya."

There was a soft beep and the apartment was slowly engulfed in silence.

She remained sitting in the dark for over ten minutes and it struck her that she'd never really noticed how silent her apartment was before. Little external noise penetrated the rooms, apart from occasional footsteps in the stairwell and the muffled sound of rush hour traffic.

With a sigh, she rose to her feet and made for the bathroom.
She left her suit and underwear in a pile on the bathroom floor and stepped into the shower. The water was hot and its pressurised needles scraped the residue of the city from her hair and body.

After the shower she returned to the lounge in a thick cotton bathrobe and sat next to a bar heater to dry her hair. Spotting the envelope on the sofa where she'd left it, she reached over and opened it. Inside, there was a Christmas card with a picture of a girl in a revealing Santa Claus suit, and another note.

Dear Miss Murphy

I'd like to take this opportunity to wish you a favourable Christmas and a peaceful new year. I'm sure you must be feeling tired after another hectic year in the corporate world. I was in London yesterday near the head office of Vitacomco when through a happy coincidence you suddenly emerged onto the street. I would have greeted you of course but I didn't want to intrude on your conversation with the young man accompanying you. I must say you both looked very happy. You were laughing and jostling one another and when he dropped his papers on the footpath the smile on your face would have launched a thousand ships. You bent down to help gather them up when your hands met over a document that you were both reaching for. You held each other's eyes for a moment but neither of you said anything.

No. This was clearly not the time to say hallo.

No doubt you'll be looking forward to your holidays by now. Perhaps you and your gentleman friend will spend some time together? I'm sure you must be very fond of him but then you always did have a thing for men in suits.

Will you miss the office while you're away, Maggie? It must be difficult to relax knowing that the cut-throat pulse of office politics continues in your absence, that you'll be unable to prevent the machinations taking place. How it must grate to know that other ambitious young women are creeping up in your shadow, poised to fill your footsteps before they've even grown cold from your passing. Some day, even you will have to accept that we can all be replaced.

But put such worries aside! Even the hardest of workers require a respite every now and again. I'm sure you won't miss the after-hours drinks with workmates, the amorous advances or the drunken confidences of colleagues at the office Christmas party. You'll hardly miss the scandalous sight of shy secretaries, grown brazen from alcohol, whipping the bras from their chests. I've heard that on such occasions corporate angels of your calibre tear off candy-striped knickers and scream with pleasure, impaled on the laps of pinstriped colleagues.

But I know these are probably little more than rumours; office tittle-tattle that brushes my ears over the years.

Merry Christmas!

She re-read the card several times with mounting apprehension. It was only when she put it aside that she realised how fast her heart was beating.

That night she slept with a chair propped against the door of her bedroom.

She did not sleep well. Her night was one interminably sinister dream of anonymous letters, unworkable deadlines, and shadowy figures whose outline could only be glimpsed from the corner of the eye. It was actually a relief when she was finally jolted awake by the peals of the telephone on the bedside table. Groggily, she reached a hand out from beneath her duvet, picked up the phone and grunted into the mouthpiece.

"Uh!"

"Maggie! Have I woken you?"

Even through the cobwebs of sleep she recognised her friend Niamh. The reassuring brogue was immediately identifiable to ears accustomed to British accents and was instantly calming, even over the miles of telephone wire.

"No," she lied. "Just dozing. How good to hear from you. Are you in London?"

"Yes. I've just arrived to do some Christmas shopping. Can you meet for coffee?"

"At Maddles?"

"Maddles would be grand. How does one o'clock suit you?"

Maggie glanced at her alarm clock.

"Sure! One o'clock's grand."

They chatted briefly, said goodbye and hung up.

She remained in bed for several minutes, recovering from the unexpected jumpstart to her weekend and the dregs of a nightmare that continued to contaminate her mood. She tried to remember the details of her dreams but was unable to recall anything other than vague shapes and a lingering unease. She shivered before bolstering her morale with the thought that her friend was in town. She nodded to herself in anticipation. Yes! She could count on Niamh for a sympathetic ear and forthright advice.

Like many strong friendships, Maggie's relationship with Niamh was founded on an intrinsic mutual empathy, consolidated by strong geographical and cultural ties. Both girls had grown up in the same small Irish town and had become best of friends in the local secondary school they'd attended. They'd registered at university together, graduated together, when they'd finally taken the plunge and left Ireland to work in London, had even shared a flat together.

In all, they'd shared accommodation in London for almost three years. In the final year, Niamh had started a relationship with an English colleague and subsequently moved out to live with him. Since then their individual paths had diverged more significantly. After a prolonged and bitter separation from his ex-wife, Niamh's partner had left the city for the 'good life' in Cornwall. Niamh had followed him shortly afterwards.

Maggie had remained in London to pursue her career.

Although she'd understood that their friendship would diminish over time, Niamh's departure had left a significant vacuum in Maggie's life. She'd lost a true friend and confidante, and for a relatively solitary person like Maggie losing such a friend was like losing a limb — neither could be easily replaced. Over the following year, the extent to which their lifestyles had changed had never been more apparent than when Maggie had travelled to Cornwall to support her friend for the birth of her first child. As she watched the proud mother cuddling her newborn daughter, she realised that although her friendship might always be valued, its intensity would never be the same again.

Apart from its effect on their relationship, time seemed to have had little other physical impact on Niamh. When she arrived at Maddles that afternoon her handsome, freckled face didn't look a day older. She still favoured the same loose, flowing dresses and ragged hairstyle that set off her attractive auburn hair to best effect. The only real difference was the addition of the baby stroller that she negotiated like a lawnmower between the chairs and tables of the family-unfriendly café.

Maggie ordered espressos as Niamh pulled her baby from the stroller and bounced her on her lap. When she returned to the table, her friend studied her closely.

"You look exhausted! Are you still burning the midnight oil for Vitacomco?"

The reminder of her fatigue made her yawn, despite herself. She smiled and shook her head.

Her friend wasn't taken in.

"Rubbish! Vitacomco doesn't promote people who aren't one hundred percent committed to the company vision. They must have you working fourteen-hour days at the very least."

"It has been hectic. I'm managing several major accounts now and the deadlines are quite rigid." She paused and sipped her coffee. "But Vitacomco isn't as bad as people make it out to be."

"John seems to think so. He contracted there a few years back and sweated blood and tears before they were satisfied. I don't know how you've lasted so long." She offered the baby to Maggie, stifling a smile as Maggie grasped the infant with the obvious discomfort of a non-parent.

"When's the last time you took a holiday?"

"About six months ago."

She released the lie without rancour even as she uttered it. Like many of the lies she'd learned to live with over the years, it rolled effortlessly off her tongue. She took the baby's hand and smiled at it. The baby burped and smiled back and something twisted deep inside her.

"She's as beautiful as her mother."

Niamh smiled, accepting the compliment gracefully. "And her father."

"How is John?"

"He's well. He doesn't miss the corporate life."

She reached over and wiped a glob of regurgitated milk from the baby's mouth with a tissue. "He's started a gardening business this year. He seems to enjoy that."

Maggie recalled the exhausted businessman who'd turned up at their flat on occasion to spend the night with her friend. She found it hard to picture that same person digging in a garden in a T-shirt and jeans, but acknowledged circumstances had been very different back then. She experienced a certain sense of embarrassment as she recalled her own excitement at her friend's illicit affair with a married man. At the time she'd been naively drawn into the delicious excitement of such forbidden adventure. It was hard to believe that, even in her youthful innocence, she could ever have considered it romantic, particularly as she now found such affairs so immensely sad and tawdry.

Niamh sipped her coffee. It left a frothy moustache on her lip that she removed with the tip of her tongue.

"You know, sometimes I think it's strange how things have worked out. We could have ended up living in the States."

Maggie nodded. Before leaving Ireland, they'd been unable to decide whether they should travel to America or to Europe via London. In the end they'd simply tossed a coin. Heads for Europe, tails for America. Heads had won.

"It's true, I suppose. If we'd gone to the States you'd never have met John. Or had a baby, for that matter."

"If we'd gone to the States, you'd probably have had four!" her friend countered and laughed.

"Ach, motherhood suits you, Niamh."

"Motherhood suits most women. It's kinda intrinsic."

"I'm serious. You look healthy, you look happy, you look …" She trailed off.

"And you?" asked Niamh. "Are you happy?"

"I've grown cold, Niamh."

The simple truth of her statement startled her. She was unused to exposing such intimate slices of her soul, even to a friend like Niamh. She lapsed into silence until she realised that her friend was observing her with concern.

"Like my coffee!" she added quickly. She smiled but it was a false smile and it turned out that, in the end, there were some lies so big even her slick tongue couldn't brush them aside, lies that lodged like a great lump in her throat and choked her smile with a bitter aftertaste.

Out in the city a siren wailed like a lost child in the confines of the high-rise buildings. The patrons of the café started as a sudden squall burst through the doors, sending a chilling gust of cold air through the room. For a moment chaos reigned as the waiters rushed to the swinging doors and struggled to hold them shut. Paper napkins were whisked up from the counter by the wind and showered around the café like a great cascade of giant white butterflies. The patrons stared, aghast, as their sanctuary was so thoughtlessly violated by the forces of nature. On Maggie's lap the baby stared at the paper napkins as they tumbled earthwards, then gurgled and squeezed her finger.

"If we'd gone to the States," she thought.

They'd been chatting for more than an hour before Maggie finally summoned up the courage to tell her friend about the cards. At first, Niamh had scoffed in open amusement.

"What! You're being stalked by correspondence?"

"Yes."

Niamh paused, taking in the utter seriousness in her friend's eyes.

"Do you have them with you?"

"No," Maggie lied. "I forgot to bring them." She felt a twinge of guilt as she pictured the letters lodged in a compartment of her handbag, but she was too embarrassed to show them to her friend.

"But I've got the envelopes!" She pulled the three envelopes from her handbag and placed them on the table, taking care not to reveal the cards as she did so.

"Hmm." Niamh chewed her lip and studied the envelopes. "Tell me about them."

So Maggie told her how she'd returned home to find the first card, the second, and the worrying escalation in the content of the third card. Too embarrassed to repeat what had actually been written in the last card, she described it in more generic, if equally powerful, terms.

"So you say these cards always arrive on a Friday?"

"That's right. God knows when they're actually posted."

"Wednesday," said Niamh without hesitation.

"What?"

"Wednesday. Look! If they're delivered on Friday that means they must be sorted for distribution by Thursday night. That suggests that they arrive from Lille on Wednesday night or Thursday morning. International airmail is restricted to strict schedules." She picked up the envelopes. "Look at the date stamps."

Maggie studied the envelopes and noted that the stamps did, indeed, bear a small date stamp that corresponded to three different Wednesdays in November and December.

"I hadn't realised mail delivery was such an exact science."

Her friend smiled, clearly enjoying the conspiracy of it all. "I temped at a British Mail sorting office a few years ago. The processes weren't so complicated that I'd forget them easily. Anyway!" She indicated another small mark on the back of the envelopes. "Look at this! Those marks show that the envelopes were delivered to the Vieux-Lille post office in Lille. The French postal service use specific codes to differentiate mail received directly at individual post offices from those collected at the various mailboxes in the city."

"Which means that whoever is sending these cards actually posts them at the Vieux-Lille post office on a Wednesday."

"That's right."

"Interesting," said Maggie.

"Isn't it?"

Maggie looked at her friend.

"Is this your way of suggesting that I travel to Vieux-Lille to see who's posting those letters?"

Niamh shrugged.

"It's probably the easiest way to unmask your mysterious stalker. After all, it must be someone you know. Who else would know your personal address?"

"Are you mad? We've no idea who this person is. He could be a raving psychopath for all we know!"

"Ach, it's hardly likely to be dangerous in the middle of a busy post office, is it? Besides, I'll be there with you. I'll get John to look after the baby and take two days off to go with you. It'll be like old times. What do you think?"

Buoyed by a double espresso and her own natural enthusiasm, Niamh sounded convincingly persuasive. Maggie breathed deeply, closed her eyes, and wished she was back in bed. She felt exhausted suddenly, harried and scared and at the same time touched by her friend's offer of assistance and the prospect of spending time together.

In her arms the baby screwed up its eyes and started to cry.

After a second lukewarm *café au lait*, Maggie decided that coming to Vieux-Lille had not been a particularly good idea. After a third, she was finally able to admit that she'd been remarkably foolish. Once again she'd allowed her friend's enthusiasm to sweep her up into an adventure she really wanted no part of.

She took another sip of the bitter coffee and, looking through the café window, recalled how rational her friend's suggestion had seemed the previous weekend. Tired and demoralised, she knew that in the end she'd allowed herself to be persuaded uniquely by the thought of some respite from the loneliness of London and the prospect of renewing an important friendship.

The first indication of any setback to the plan had been a message on her answering machine the following Tuesday night. Maggie had listened with increasing disillusionment as Niamh's recorded voice explained that she wasn't going to be able to accompany her to Lille. Through the profuse apologies, Maggie was able to make out that her baby had come down with a virus and required her presence and support.

So do I, she'd thought miserably.

She'd immediately admonished herself for such a reaction. It was only natural, she told herself, that her friend should put her baby's welfare ahead of hers. And yet, even as she justified it, Maggie could not help the empty feeling that seemed to swell inside her, the conviction that something had irreconcilably changed and things would never be the same between her and Niamh again.

She tossed and turned in bed throughout the night, wondering whether to go to Lille on her own or to simply relinquish the whole undertaking. Her first instinct had been to forget the whole idea. Unfortunately, the ticket had already been paid for. More importantly, she'd managed to book three days leave from work, a feat that had cost her dearly in promises and future favours. At two in the morning, following five hours of restless contemplation, she finally made the decision to proceed as planned. Shortly afterwards, sleep crept up on her and caught her unawares.

In the cold light of day it didn't take long to regret her decision. It was raining when she'd boarded the TGV at Waterloo station and by the time she'd arrived in Lille the weather had deteriorated even further. A bitter wind howled through the streets, driving the rain ahead of it in blusteringly saturated squalls and for several moments she remained at the entrance to the station, tempted to let it all go and board the next train back to London. In the end, however, an inner streak of resolution had manifested itself and she found herself stepping out into the whirling storm.

It didn't take Maggie long to locate the Vieux-Lille post office. In this she was greatly helped by the flashy modern architecture of the building, a design that immediately distinguished it from the buildings surrounding it. Inside, the service area for outgoing and international mail turned out to be surprisingly restricted. Containing little more than a single counter, two service *guichets* and a small stall with information pamphlets, the room was completely bare and clearly unsuitable for any form of discreet surveillance. There was nowhere that Maggie could scrutinise the people entering the service area without being seen. Remaining there for any period of time without a clear objective would also arouse the suspicions of the clientele and the staff behind the service counter.

Frustrated, Maggie had hurried from the building and fled to a café across the street.

Catching the waiter's eye, Maggie used sign language to order another espresso. As the waiter walked away the disdain on his features was reflected in the window of the café. Embarrassed, she glanced around and was disturbed to find several of the patrons staring openly at her. Most looked away when she caught their eye. One or two, more brazen, smiled condescendingly at her before returning their attention to their food.

Thoughts in disarray, Maggie focused on a complimentary copy of the local paper and pretended to study it, although she understood little French. It took her several minutes to work out why she was a source of such interest and, even then, this was uniquely as a result of catching her own reflection in the café window. A black business suit, the grey, '60s-style mackintosh, hair flattened by the rain. In preparation for her trip that morning she'd unconsciously attired herself like the female lead from a black-and-white gangster movie. Sitting alone with a cigarette in hand, gazing out at the rain-drenched streets, had only enhanced the comparison with some character from a second-rate *film noir*. Bristling, she stubbed her cigarette out and ignored the waiter's smirk as he deposited the coffee on her table. Pulling a barrette from her pocket, she tightened her hair into the formal bun normally reserved for the office.

She felt a rush of revulsion for it all: the café, the waiter, the city, and most intensely for the faceless correspondent responsible for her presence there. As drops of rain congealed and flowed down the windowpanes, she stared across at the post office and wondered how she could have been so naive. She'd wasted time and money, travelling in the middle of winter to a city she didn't know, to identify a person she'd probably never seen before. In truth, she had achieved nothing more than to make herself the laughing stock of the local dining fraternity.

Across the road more evidence of her naivety taunted her. Her panic-driven choice for surveillance could hardly have been less effective. Although she could see people enter and leave through the main entrance of the post office, due to the heavy rainfall the majority of them were wearing hats or carried umbrellas that obscured their faces. She sighed and shook her head. The whole pathetic, misguided plan had been an unmitigated disaster!

It was time to go home.

As she gathered up her few belongings, two individuals approached the post office and she glanced at them with waning interest. The first, a solidly built labourer, had covered his head with his jacket. The second, a well-dressed woman in her early fifties, pulled a selection of letters from an expensive leather handbag in the shelter of the main entrance. Neither looked to be the type to send abusive mail to a stranger in another country. Turning away from the window, she stood up to leave, then stiffened.

Hurrying from the café, she rushed to a discreet spot near the post office from where she could watch the entrance without being seen. Hunched and shivering against the rain, she waited until the woman re-emerged and walked away in the direction of the city centre. Maintaining a short distance between them, Maggie followed close behind.

The woman slowly strolled through Vieux-Lille beneath the shelter of a wide golf umbrella while Maggie, growing progressively wetter, vainly sought refuge under the intermittent canopies of various shops and boutiques. She was relieved when the woman finally halted at a café on Rue Esquermoise. Sheltering in the entrance of a small apartment block, Maggie brushed the worst of the raindrops from her hair. She watched as the woman took a terrace seat that was sheltered from the rain by an overhanging canopy and ordered a drink from the garçon.

Maggie waited for the order to be served before leaving her refuge and approaching the woman's table. The woman looked up in surprise as she realised someone was standing before her.

"Do you know who I am?"

The woman stared at her and Maggie watched as the expression on her face transformed from surprise to undisguised loathing.

"I know who you are. Do you know who I am?"

She hadn't been absolutely sure but the clipped English accent confirmed it.

"Yes. I didn't know you lived in France, but I saw your face in a photo once. I have a very good memory."

"If a poor taste in men."

She ignored that.

"May I sit down?"

"Do I have any choice?"

"Not really."

Maggie took a seat at the table.

The woman pointedly ignoring her, and pulled a packet of cigarettes and a gold-plated lighter from her handbag. Her hand shook as she lit a cigarette and the clinking of her bangles and bracelets sounded inordinately loud in the strained silence between them.

"I realised who you were when I noticed one of the letters you were pulling from your handbag had a pale yellow envelope. Were you sending that to me?"

The woman regarded her coldly.

"I'd like you to stop writing to me. An occasional letter is usually welcome but I can do without yours."

The woman exhaled a cloud of smoke across the table at Maggie.

"You know, I still have a pair of your knickers. A red pair of silk panties."

"I doubt it. I only wear black or white knickers."

The woman gave no indication that she'd even been listening.

"He always was a knickers man. That's how I found out about you. They were in the pocket of his suit, a touching souvenir of some wild night's activity, no doubt! I followed him from the office the next day. He'd told me he was going to a business conference in Brighton but he was actually going to your apartment. Quite careless, really."

She pulled on the cigarette again. Maggie found herself sickened by the sucking, almost slurping, sound she made. It sounded as though she was actually drinking the nicotine.

"Perhaps he wanted you to find them."

"I've always wondered what kind of woman would wear red silk panties."

"I wouldn't know. As I said, I only wear black or white."

"To celebrate a chequered career in the corporate world, no doubt!" She smiled bitterly and blew another cloud of smoke across the table. "I see you've being doing inordinately well at Vitacomco. You must have fucked half the office to get that far." She sneered but even as it dissipated, traces of the expression remained in the lines and wrinkles of her face. It was as though the residue of a lifetime's worth of poisonous thoughts had permanently engraved their outline into her features.

"You really are a venomous bitch, aren't you?"

"And you're really nothing more than a home-breaking little whore, are you!"

Maggie sighed and shook her head.

"You haven't picked up on the fact that those weren't my knickers, have you? I mean it hasn't actually clicked that you're talking to the wrong woman, that I didn't have an affair with your husband."

The woman snorted and sucked noisily on her cigarette again.

"You're a liar! You can always tell a liar from the eyes and I can tell you're a true professional."

Something inside Maggie snapped. Without warning she reached across the table and plucked the cigarette from the woman's hand.

"Let's put out that nasty cigarette."

"How dare y …"

And Maggie slapped her across the face.

For a moment the older woman's mouth actually hung open in astonishment. Maggie took advantage of the pause to pull a small photograph of Niamh, her partner, and her baby from her bag and held it up before her. For a moment she thought the woman was going to scream with outrage but as her eyes fell on the photo the scream fluttered and died soundlessly on her lips.

"It was my flatmate," said Maggie. "You followed your husband to the right flat, but you got the wrong person."

The woman continued to stare, transfixed, at the photograph. To

Maggie it appeared as though she'd just folded up inside. She no longer looked mean or formidable, just old and lonely.

"They have a baby!" The voice was hollow, the words so faint that Maggie could barely hear them.

"Yes. They have a baby. But they don't deserve to receive abuse from you. Quite frankly, neither do I."

She replaced the photo in her bag and stood up to go. On a sudden impulse she turned back to face the woman. "Why?" she asked.

"What?" The woman barely glanced at her. Her eyes were very far away.

"Why did you start writing those poisonous letters? After all these years."

The woman looked at her blankly, as though unable to comprehend the question, then the expression on her face collapsed in on itself. A low gasp escaped her lips and her body shuddered in a series of deep, wrenching sobs.

Maggie stared in astonishment but before she could gather her thoughts the woman jumped to her feet and rushed from the table. She could only watch, dumbfounded, as the small figure tottered away into a fresh downpour. Her outline quickly disappeared from sight but even the noise of rain could not cloak the haunting cries of despair that echoed back along the street.

Back at the station, Maggie decided to return to London in business class. And to charge the cost to Vitacomco.

It was unlike her to act so rebelliously but the encounter with John's ex-wife had shaken her. Unused to such confrontation, she felt an instinctive need to withdraw, to isolate herself as far as possible from her fellow passengers.

As the train pulled away from the quay she settled into her seat and did her best to relax, but the events in Lille continued to gnaw beneath her tranquil demeanour. At first she tried to trivialise what had happened, dismissing the woman's actions as nothing more than those of a deeply disturbed person, of yet another lost soul. Deep down, however, deep in the recesses of the soul where the truth is instinctively exposed, she knew that that was just another lie. The experience in Lille had unravelled a thread inside her. No matter how much she attempted to rationalise the naked hatred of a vicious woman, she knew that if the layers of venom were peeled away a loneliness and despair very similar to her own would be revealed. This was her true fear. The unforeseen trip to Lille had temporarily diverted her from the trajectory of her current existence and gave her a terrifying glimpse of her potential future. In Lille she had recognised a kindred lost soul. She knew it was no longer possible to resume the course her life had been taking, to carry on lying as though nothing had happened.

Her thoughts were interrupted by the sound of the carriage door opening and she glanced down the aisle where a pair of enterprising mime artists, a young man and a woman with white faces and bowler hats, had somehow gained access to business class. Taking immediate advantage of their captive audience, the girl placed her bowler hat upside-down in the middle of the aisle and they commenced an impromptu performance for their more moneyed fellow passengers. Maggie looked away towards the window to find her reflection staring back at her, studying her with an aggressive expression. For one second, through some trick of the light or the shimmering reflection of some object in the background she saw the face of the other woman superimposed on her own. Then, just as quickly, it was gone and she was staring at a woman in a strict business suit and tight black hair who looked vaguely familiar but whom she'd never really seen before.

She released her hair and as the curls bounced down around her shoulders it seemed to her that, although her own lips hadn't moved, her reflection smiled back at her. She turned away and, pulling a sheet of paper from her handbag, spent the next ten minutes composing a letter of resignation to Vitacomco. For the remainder of the journey, she watched the mime artists perform in grinding slow motion as the world hurtled past, oblivious, on either side.

Suddenly, a valley

They say Dad's hand was reaching for his favourite cassette when the car crashed through the barrier and plunged into the valley. The music he'd been searching for had been an album by Edith Piaf — *Soudain, une vallée*.

Or so the story goes.

Over the years I've thought about it in great depth. I've examined and analysed it, considered it from every possible angle without coming any closer to understanding how the accident happened. Sometimes the truth can be as elusive as a whisper in an echoing stairwell and in this particular case, no matter which way you looked, you always ended up with more questions than answers. Why had it been so important for Dad to hear that cassette? Why hadn't he waited? A few seconds and he'd have cleared the bend, returning to a flat stretch leading away from the cliff. What had he been thinking when he'd looked up and saw the road had disappeared? And the windscreen flaring, full and green, with fatal vegetation?

To this day the only thing I'm really certain of is that I don't place much faith in that particular story. There are too many facts that cannot be ignored; documented facts typed in official 12-point font, copied in triplicate, filed and archived. Most of these facts disproved what was, in essence, nothing more than local folklore and yet the story would turn up again every few years or so, resurfacing like a drowned body that refuses to sink.

Due to the roughness of the terrain it took the rescuers over three hours to work their way down to the wreckage. As they clambered down the steep slopes they could hear the car stereo still going. Although the vehicle was battered and crushed against a pine tree at the bottom of the cliff, the battery and the cassette player had somehow survived the plunge intact. Piaf's throaty voice continued to waft through the hills, haunting the wildlife until the battery ran out. The topography of the valley floor formed a natural auditorium that amplified the music and sent it spinning down to the lowlands to scare the livestock of local farmers. People still remember the bitter milk that leaked from the udders of those cows for several days after.

Thirty years later I can always tell when the story's back. When Maggie and I step into our local tavern the conversation falters and people look down into their beer as though searching for some resonant secret in the swirling liquid. I tell Maggie that it doesn't really bother me. People need stories like that, yarns and legends that give them the opportunity to shake their heads, shrug and sigh with practised resignation.

I don't allow the story to touch me any more, for if Dad had been reaching for the cassette then it was hardly likely to have been playing when the rescuers arrived.

Unless he managed to insert it as he hurtled through the fence, and over the precipice, into the green layer of foliage below.

Maggie does her best to shield me from the story but you can't stop people talking, particularly drunks or loudmouths who blush when they notice me standing behind them. Meanwhile, the story keeps going. Like Edith Piaf. Until the battery finally died.

After the accident my mum, red-eyed and pale, had told me that Dad had gone to heaven. I was six at the time, struggling with the concept that he'd needed to take the car to get there, but I still remember the sickly sensation that came with comprehension. The strange thing was that although Mum was obviously grieving, I had the feeling there was more to the story than she was telling me.

From that day on Mum rarely talked of Dad again, but my sisters and I knew that, despite the silence, she still suffered. Sometimes, years later, despair could suddenly engulf her and knock her to her knees as she erupted in a fit of tears. My sisters and I would discuss such events over secret late-night meetings, shaking our heads solemnly and tut-tutting like adults.

After the funeral, everyone came back to the house to eat and to mumble platitudes. Father Byrne, our priest, gave me the cassette that had been retrieved from the wreckage. I kept it under my bed in my treasure box with my Star Wars card collection, my catapult and various rocks and shells. On nights when I couldn't sleep I'd examine it by torchlight, imagining Dad's fingers stretched around it as his car ripped through the undergrowth. Sometimes I'd dream I was in the back seat as he drove along the cliff road. I'd watch as he neared the bend and looked down to reach over to the glove compartment. His fingers would close around the cassette when he realised he'd driven off the side of the road. As the car smashed through the fence he would start to scream and I'd wake up to realise that it was me who was screaming.

I had these nightmares from time to time but lately they've become more frequent. Maggie's been very supportive, always there to hold me as I lie gasping for breath as though I'd run a marathon. It hasn't been easy for Maggie. Fifteen years of waking up at night to comfort our three girls, more recently our little boy, and now, just when things have finally settled down she gets woken up for me.

Both of my sisters married and moved away to the city. They still come back occasionally but even those rare visits have dwindled. It's odd, but whenever they do come home, although we'll talk for hours about our mother, we never mention Dad. It's as though after the funeral we folded up all our memories of him and locked them away in a dusty attic.

It wasn't always like that. For months after the funeral we'd play games, pretending he was still alive, drawing pictures of him and sticking them on our walls. Sometimes we'd just stare at his empty place at the breakfast table and say nothing.

Memories of Dad continue to pop into my head at the strangest times, seizing my thoughts like dirt in a cog. Once, during my ninth birthday, when I bent down to blow out the candles on my cake, he was suddenly in my head and I didn't have any breath left. Tears burned my eyes and a lump of phlegm lodged like a small rock in the back of my throat. I started to blubber, rocking back and forth as I huddled deeper and deeper into myself. My school friends looked on, wide-eyed as I was led away to my room. Later, as I lay on my bed, I could hear their laughter as their parents came to collect them and take them home.

The vacuum of Dad's absence seemed to increase rather than diminish as I grew older, but it was only through getting older that I came to understand how much I'd loved him. It became something of an obsession for me to find people who'd known him so that I could ask them questions about him. This turned out to be surprisingly difficult. When pressed, old workmates would simply sigh and say he'd been a kind man and a hard worker. Father Byrne, clearing his throat, would look away from me, mumbling that he'd been a good man and a good father.

My own memories substantiated what other people told me. I could still see his smile as he played with me or comforted me after a fall. Although at times he seemed tired or sad, I knew this was due to his working so hard on the farm trying to raise a family. Before she stopped talking about him, Mum used to say that when Dad wasn't tired he was grumpy. But even when he was grumpy I knew Dad loved me.

My favourite memory of Dad is from when I was five and he'd been holding me in his arms, swinging me around the room, laughing that big laugh of his and even though I was terrified, I laughed because he was laughing too. On that occasion I remember that he'd suddenly placed me gently on the ground and started to cry, brushing my face softly with his hand and whispering, "My little boy! My little boy!'

I continued to pray for Dad until I reached my early teens and began resenting that God had stolen him from me. Then I became a born-again agnostic.

Mum died twelve years after Dad and on my nineteenth birthday I took my first job in the freezing works. It was there that I met Maggie and, in time, started a family of my own. Maggie could tell I was still hurting from my father's accident and tried to get me to talk about it, but it turned out I was my mother's son. I refused to discuss it until finally Maggie just gave up trying.

I hated the works but it helped pay the mortgage on the family house and after a few years I was lucky enough to get promoted to foreman. The paypacket got a little thicker but I still had to supplement our income with a part-time job helping out at the local garage. I'd return home after twelve-hour shifts to find dirty nappies, grocery bills, crying kids waiting to be washed, and other domestic chores awaiting me. On the weekends there were always repairs to do on the house, wood to chop, the vegetable garden to tame. By the time I got to bed every night I was as tired and grumpy as my father used to be.

Over the last few years, things have changed between Maggie and me. We used to laugh a lot and I remember a time when everything between us was fresh and exciting. Now there doesn't seem to be anything between us but dead space. Sometimes we close the door to the children's bedroom so that we can argue and release all the broken glass and razor blades we've been storing up inside. To avoid the arguments we've started evading each other's company, reducing our communication to snatches of conversation in the hall or left in my wake as I leave for work in the morning.

After a particularly violent argument Maggie will drive away to stay with her parents, half an hour up the valley. I spit after her, confused whether I hate her for running away or resent that I've nobody to run away to. The burden of bills, kids, a job you hate and a woman who no longer loves you can drag you into bleak places and sometimes I dream about running away, packing up the van and disappearing to a place where I could start again. I know they'll never be anything but dreams. I love my kids too much to ever leave them like that, particularly my little boy. I couldn't let him grow up to be mocked by schoolboy jokes about absent fathers.

There never seems to be enough time to empty your head and let the routine poisons of a failed existence drip out. Two weeks ago, I woke up to discover that I was almost forty. Dust had settled in the creases in my forehead and when I stepped out of the bed I could almost hear the wet squelch as I sank deeper into the mire of domestic drudgery.

Lately I've taken to jumping in the jeep without telling anybody where I'm going, driving aimlessly for hours around the hills and backblocks. Sometimes I wander up to the mountains, to the cliff road where Dad drove off the edge. Up there it's so high you can almost taste the clouds on your tongue. You can see individual squalls sweep through fields of maize further down the valley, caressing the harvest with the softness of a lover's hand.

I can sit for hours by the wooden railing, tossing tins full of stones off the cliff and listening as they crash down through the rock and undergrowth. Eventually, with some effort, I get up to go home, dreading the thought of Maggie and her serrated tongue, waiting to tear me apart.

Tonight, after another vitriolic exchange, I rush to the jeep and drive away, speeding through the dark, clocking the blackness hurtling past on either side. I'm seething, exhaling my fury through the tyres, melting the tarmac beneath. I drive for hours, turning the volume of the stereo up as high as it will go and howling along with the noise. When the fury finally fades, when it finally eases to a thumping, red glow inside my head, I realise that I'm back on the cliff road, sitting in neutral at the place where Dad went over.

In the glare of the headlights the sharpness of the bend makes it look as though the road ends at the lip of the cliff. The dotted white line runs off into the dark like a runway. Revving the engine, I can feel the power of the motor trembling in anticipation, waiting to be released, to burst forth and leap into the abyss. Beyond the timber fence the darkness is seductive. As I stare into it I finally understand that the story haunting me has never really been important and the only thing that ever really mattered was that Dad has always been there, waiting for me.

Slither

Joe the Doorman has always admired my skill with the ladies. A Neanderthal figure with a forehead as wide as a wooden plank, I often feel his eyes on me when I work the crowd. I try not to dwell on my achievements but I have to admit to an unblemished reputation when it comes to the art of professional seduction. Indeed, in all my years, there's been but a single incident to mar an otherwise spotless career — a trivial 'one-nighter' with a Polynesian darling back in the early days. Back then I'd been young and foolish and so consumed by my ardour that I'd forgotten to take the appropriate precautions.

After that liaison, there had been rumours of a physical consequence but fortunately nothing had ever eventuated. The young woman in question left Wellington shortly after our night of passion and we were never to cross paths again.

Needless to say, I learn from my mistakes and this is one of the reasons I've retained the title of 'Senior Consort' at *Pollyanna's Palace* for over two decades. *Pollyanna's* is the club where I flare into being each Saturday night. It is a nightclub of tailored suits and cocktail dresses, of subdued lighting and subtly changing shadows. A club where conversation flows like treacle, capturing rich accents in its sticky imbroglio, where leather barstools fart when you sit on them and high-class hookers quote Shakespeare for kicks.

Tonight, however, an indefinable gloom haunts the festivities and contaminates everything it touches. The nuts at the bar are stale, the Bloody Marys haemophilic. The triffid-like salad bites back when you taste it. Even the habitual Saturday night crowd seem cowed, sipping their cocktails listlessly.

"Quiet night, Mr Carlyle."

I nod to Joe the Doorman. Temporarily relieved from his duties, he is sipping a coffee behind the Venetian Bar.

"Never fear, Joe. Things will pick up."

The words have barely escaped my lips before my own divination fulfils itself. A breathtakingly beautiful Maori girl steps through the doors in a dress so tight you can see the outline of her ribs when she breathes. Time stands still as she surveys the dance floor bustle. She turns to greet a blonde girlfriend and I swallow my cocktail in anticipatory relish.

Needless to say, my less vigilant colleagues fail to note her appearance for several crucial seconds, more than sufficient time for someone of my stature to devise a suitable strategy for approaching her.

Ah, yes. My colleagues.

More 'competitors' than colleagues, even the title 'competitor' is probably too kind. They're lower-class hustlers, kerb-crawlers with pretensions of grandeur. When they eventually catch sight of the Maori girl there's a chorus of gasps, an inhaling of jelly guts and a puffing out of chests. Shaking my head at this gauche display, I inhale on an ivory-filtered cigarette and calmly blow the competition away.

Like a narcissistic boy scout, I am always prepared. My tie is silk, my suit Versace. My shoes are Gucci. Dressed to kill, I stalk my prey by creeping up on their blindside. I move confidently in shadows, walk close to walls and conceal my conscience in a cork-stopped bottle buried deep in the earth where nobody will ever find it.

I descend to the dance floor and my fellow gigolos (a shivering line of excited mohair and unsettling polyester ties) retreat acquiescently from my path.

All except, Marcini.

Ah, Marcini!

It's difficult not to be bitter about Marcini. Standing there in a white suit and a black cloak, he strives for a nonchalant air but ends up looking like some kind of confused superhero. Not that there's anything heroic about Marcini. A country boy from the Wairarapa backblocks, he recently changed his name by deed poll under the illusion that it would give a more sophisticated 'Mediterranean' air — albeit one with a Kiwi accent. Once my worthy apprentice, Marcini is now the pretender to my throne. And yet, although he's my greatest failure, I can't help feeling a certain pride at having done such a good job with him. His lines are competent and well delivered, his boyish good looks marred only by a palpable air of latent cruelty; a character flaw that's difficult to dissimulate.

A rare reptile, that Marcini. God's own gift and women's nemesis, he slinks when not slithering.

The Maori girl orders cocktails while her friend makes for the powder room. I slide into action, for quarry is best approached when isolated in unfamiliar territory. Ill at ease and alone, they are more susceptible to the lines we throw like olive branches in their path.

I glide towards her, watching cautiously from the corner of my eye as Marcini oozes with similar intent across the faded lino. Professional that I am, I've already plotted my course, setting my pace to intercept her mere seconds before Marcini's arrival — an additional snub I cannot resist.

"Hugo!"

Pollyanna, empress of the night and proprietor of the establishment, steps directly into my path, forcing me to a graceless halt. Although her hand on my arm has all the weight of a desiccated feather, it shackles me as securely as a metal chain. *La grande dame* of inner city nightlife, Pollyanna is well into her seventies but continues to rule her domain with an iron fist.

"Pollyanna, the hunt is afoot!"

"Hugo, I must insist."

"But ..."

"Hugo, darling. Even our most senior staff must adhere to the rules."

Pollyanna's face is alabaster white, her lips a thin line of purple. Her stare has all the emotional depth of a dead fish. I cloak my frustration beneath a benevolent smile. From the corner of my eye I can see that Marcini (curse him!) has beaten me to the girl as a result of Pollyanna's intrusion.

"Hugo, I wish to discuss last night's squabble between your colleagues in the Venetian lounge. Such brawls are too vulgar for the subtle tastes of my clientele. They cannot be tolerated."

"Pollyanna, I must protest! Established etiquette remained unbreached. Besides, such verbal fisticuffs are the highpoint of our careers, the culmination of our years at the barstools. We live for such moments: the barbed throwaways, the cut and thrust of bitchy wit, the succulent one-liners."

Pollyanna sniffs disdainfully.

"Don't sulk, Hugo. It makes you look like a petulant child. There will be no further discussion. You'll simply inform your colleagues of my decision and the matter will end there." Raising a dampened handkerchief, she dabs one dried out tear duct. "And for God's sake, Hugo, try to be more civil to young Marcini. He'll fill your shoes effectively one day."

I bow acquiescently as she makes her royal exit in a flurry of rustling lace. Pollyanna is, after all, queen of the temple and I am but a temporary champion. Even a person of my unsurpassed vanity understands there must come a day when my reign as 'favourite' will draw to a close, when I must fall nobly on my sword or go down fighting the rush of treacherous gigolos slithering in to fill my place.

But Marcini! Fill my shoes! The only way Marcini will ever fill these shoes is if I mince him and pour him in, piece by messy piece!

Smouldering with resentment, I wander towards the Safari Bar where Marcini and the two young women are engaged in animated conversation. Oblivious to my presence, the blonde girl laughs loudly, amused by one of Marcini's anecdotes. Marcini smiles indulgently, confident of getting what he wants. He likes to claim that he was born with a silver spoon in his mouth but the truth is he's equally well equipped with a razor wit and a forked tongue. The man is a veritable Swiss army knife of distasteful characteristics.

I linger sullenly in the shadow but, despite my frustration, avoid any open demonstration of hostility. Marcini's status in Pollyanna's Palace is, after all, an embarrassing testament to my own lack of judgement.

Two years earlier, in anticipation of my eventual retirement, I had commenced a proactive selection process for a suitable successor. Deceived by his false sincerity and weasel words of flattery, I'd chosen Marcini above the other candidates.

To be repaid with treachery!

Unwilling to partake in the rigorous apprenticeship I'd so carefully designed, Marcini had unexpectedly rebelled, approaching Pollyanna to plead his case and even going so far as offering to take my place. Although impressed by such unbridled ambition, Pollyanna had rejected his proposal. To my dismay, however, she had agreed to give him the official designation of 'senior escort in-waiting'.

Biting my tongue, I had made no complaint. Nevertheless, I knew I'd never forgive Marcini's deceit. I would not forget that, like Merlin, I'd been deceived and almost usurped by the ambitions of my acolyte.

My decision to intrude on the little group is a hasty move, spurred by pique and childish petulance. Marcini has his back to me as I slip out of the shadows and insert myself neatly beside him. It's a slick manoeuvre — smooth and just within the house rules, but it's still a close thing. By interfering with the seduction of a colleague's prey I am flouting the established etiquette. Professionally, I am on the razor's edge.

"Good evening."

Marcini spins around in astonishment.

"Hugo! How good of you to join us."

His velvet drawl belies the poisonous look in his eyes.

"Marcini," I nod pleasantly.

"Good evening," says the Maori girl.

I stare openly at her. Her gaze is direct, her smile sincere. Her conversation is free of artifice, her face of makeup. Her dress is simple but it's very simplicity amplifies her beauty. It is little wonder that cynical eyes are drawn to her for she is as pure as an untainted spring.

"I was just saying what a beautiful city you live in," says the girl. "I'd always thought our valley in Northland was the most beautiful place on Earth but it's nothing compared with the sophistication of Wellington. I haven't travelled much," she adds with a shy smile.

Startled, I momentarily wonder if she's mocking me. Forthright expression is a commodity so rare in Pollyanna's Palace it could almost be considered extinct. Even Marcini looks surprised. You can almost see his ham-handed thoughts lumbering around in the back of his head as he struggles to adapt to such unexpected honesty. Almost by default he settles for the 'wise but sensitive' approach.

"Yes, it is a beautiful city. Have you seen the lights from Mt Victoria at night? The view is ..." he pauses for effect, "... exquisite."

"Tell me about your valley," I ask the girl, shuffling Marcini's inanity aside, instinctively honing in on what's important.

"My valley? Oh, it's just a valley with rolling green hills. Our farm's on the side of one hill and also looks over the ocean. Every morning when I open the curtains I'm struck by the impact of aquatic blue.'

She flicks her head in an unconscious gesture that is shockingly familiar. I experience a sudden horrible sensation of having somehow fallen outside myself; as though I'm floating above the group like a party balloon trapped in the ceiling rafters.

Ignorant of my predicament, the girl chats happily while my empty body looks on, slack-jawed and vacant. The blonde girl nods earnestly in agreement while Marcini, standing to one side, glowers like a predator chased from the choicest entrails of its kill.

I gaze at her helplessly. Despite her beauty I can already feel my intent draining away, the carnal spark snuffed like a smothered flame.

In the end it's Marcini who brings me back to earth. He's always had a marvellous way of knocking one down from lofty heights.

"I beg your pardon, Marcini! What did you say?"

"Is your hearing going, Hugo? I said, isn't it a little late for you. Shouldn't you be at home in your slippers with a hot cocoa?"

"I'm a social professional, Marcini. Not a university don. You'd know the difference if you'd ever passed third form."

"Please," says the girl. "Please don't argue."

Her obvious concern is sufficient to silence us both. I glance at Marcini, disturbed to see the hunger swelling in his eyes. At that moment I realise I'm not going to let him have her, that I cannot let him tear this girl's soul apart.

I appreciate, of course, that such grandiose thoughts are all a little absurd where I'm concerned. At my age, it's a little late to start repenting my sins and rediscovering God, or Buddha, or whoever else is lurking down there in the recesses of my soul. This reality has never caused me a moment's moral reticence.

Until tonight.

Until this individual uncorks the bottle.

And the limits of my immorality are revealed.

Despite the encumbrance of my newfound moral burden, I immediately start to monopolise the conversation, deliberately leading it to subjects where Marcini is weakest. As the night wears on his frustration mounts as he finds himself with less and less to say. When the girls excuse themselves for another visit to the powder room he immediately turns on me.

"What are you up to, Hugo?"

"Why nothing, Marcini."

His lips turn up in an almost reptilian snarl and I'm struck by the enamel gleam of his incisors. Marcini is a natural predator. Despite my unruffled façade he can sense I'm encumbered by some rare handicap. Leaning against the bar, he appraises me carefully over the lip of his cocktail, determined to identify my weakness.

"She's mine, Hugo. I saw her first."

He's guessing. Instinctively closing in on my Achilles heel. Nevertheless, it's simply a matter of time before he works it out.

I understand then that to save the Maori girl I will have no option but to flout the house rules, to create a distraction that will divert Marcini's attention from her to me.

I light a cigarette and consider him dispassionately before responding.

"No, Marcini. I saw her first. You were drooling over the bar whores until you noticed everyone staring gob-smacked in her direction."

"I approached her first, Hugo. You're encroaching on my territory. You know the rules prohibit such interference."

I have to laugh at that.

"Yes, Marcini. I do know the rules. I wrote them. Unfortunately …" I shrug helplessly, "… my regrettable lapse does impact on your interaction. Any interruption in the initial fifteen minutes of contact significantly reduces the chances of carnal success. Or have you forgotten everything I've taught you?"

"You pompous ass! If it wasn't for your intrusion she'd be eating out of my hand!"

"A poor excuse, Marcini."

"An excuse!" The pitch of Marcini's voice is decidedly higher. "You create your own standards and then proceed to ignore them when you can't meet them. How typical of you, you pompous capon!"

The light from the powder room door glows in the corner of my eye. It's time to go for the jugular.

"At least I'm a professional, Marcini. You'll never be anything but a second-rate pimp with all the panache of a wet fart. Forget the girl. She's well beyond your reach."

"She's still within my reach, you old windbag!"

"Oh, really? What are you going to do? Walk up and give her a hongi?"

He actually snarls at me and raises his fist.

"Such short-lived respect for the rules, Marcini! You know Pollyanna abhors violence within the establishment."

"Are you trying to be smart, old man?"

"I am smart. I was being flippant."

"I'll flippin …"

I never see his fist coming, never even feel the impact. One moment I'm standing serenely, the next, I'm lying crumpled on the scuffed lino.

The girl arrives just in time to witness Marcini's furious reaction and gapes at him with horrified eyes. Even as he stands there expelling expletives, he knows he's blown it.

Across the dance floor, Pollyanna is watching us with frosty hostility. Seeing the expression on my face, Marcini follows my gaze to where Pollyanna stands regarding him with equal enmity and finally realises that I've dragged him over the precipice with me.

"You bastard!"

He spits the words out, supporting this conclusion with an unanticipated kick to my head.

I just have time to see the bouncers take him down before everything fades away.

I regain my senses on a sofa in the foyer by the staff entrance. Joe the Doorman, sitting silently beside me, nods amiably when he sees me stir.

Soft music emanates through the swinging doors but the foyer is eerily deserted. There's no sign of my colleagues, no Maori girl, nobody to comfort poor, self-sacrificing Hugo. My head droops as I recall the look on Pollyanna's face. I'm an ostracised figure now. Stripped of all honours, I am unwelcome on the premises and must farewell those privileges I've always taken for granted: my bar-tab, my customised barstool, unlimited finger food.

I shake my head and sadly turn to consider Joe.

"There was a girl here earlier, Joe. A Polynesian darling."

Wrinkles form on Joe's broad forehead then his face cracks open to reveal a surprisingly winsome smile.

"Ah, yes! White dress." He sighs. "She left after all the commotion but she was very friendly. Said her mother used to come here back in the old days and had met her father here."

"That's right, Joe. Back in the old days."

My head aches and I can taste blood in my mouth. The left side of my face is swollen and for the first time in my life I feel no need to locate a mirror. Joe's expression was sympathetic.

"The other clubs would only be too happy to have you, Mr Carlyle." he says.

I shake his hand before departing.

"Goodnight, Joe."

"Goodnight, Mr Carlyle."

I strive to feel gallant as I leave Pollyanna's Palace but the brutal closure to my reign has shaken me. Despite Joe's well-intentioned words

I know there can never be any other clubs, for I'll always be tempted by young Polynesian darlings and I'll always stare into their hazel eyes and wonder if …

I pretend to bask in new-found morality as I weave through lonely city streets, but deep down I'm not fooling anyone. It would be nice to wrap myself in robes of self-righteousness as I wander off into the sunset but the truth is that this leopard's too much of a shit to ever change his spots.

Chuckling cynically, I slip into the shadows as the first embers of dawn glow on the Orongorongo hills.

And flee the brightness of the incoming day.

Cinema

FADE IN

I*t starts with a whirring* and a flickering light. A dark screen. A man's voice.

BUTLER: Miss Dalloway!

A sudden view of the back of a woman's head. The head turns towards the camera for a close-up of the most perfect female features. Rich, red lips. Dimples like dents in the side of her cheeks. Piercing blue eyes with a trace of smudged fatigue. Long dark hair curling over the collar of her business suit. Thick, and black as an oil slick.

MISS DALLOWAY: Yes?

BUTLER: I have a message. A message from Sir Russell in London.

And that's how it begins. *The Hideaway*. It is my favourite movie.

The Hideaway is a classic slice of contemporary cinema. It bears a script that is erudite and relevant, and cinematography that finally reveals the true grandeur of the southern English coastline. It is a visual gem, a rare jewel whose brilliance shines out from the other dross appearing on our screens all too often these days.

The movie's success lies in its simplicity. Miss Julia Dalloway, a businesswoman with a heart of gold, is tired of the rat race in the big city. Tired of the rodent hordes, the little people, who swarm the streets far below her penthouse. Beneath her *haute-couture*, Miss Dalloway is a woman of plain tastes. She enjoys the simple things in life. She longs for nothing more than to retire to grow roses in a Devonshire country cottage. And to meet a true gentleman to whom she can give her love.

And live happily ever after.

In the movie, Miss Dalloway meets several suitors of varying pedigree and status. None of them can help but fall madly in love with her, but the majority lust predominantly after her riches. Needless to say, a woman of Miss Dalloway's calibre and breeding can see through them all.

The film ends rather sadly. As the camera draws back she is revealed in her drawing room, a lonely, yet debonair figure, sitting by the fire and listening to the weather forecast. Even in her sadness, she remains a wonderful figure of feminine dignity. "Yes!" she says. "Tomorrow will be a lovely day."

My girlfriend says that my deep affection for this movie is an unhealthy obsession. I cannot, in all honestly, agree with her. Although it's true I have the video, the poster, the DVD, the soundtrack, the script, the screenplay, and the original book on which the screenplay was based — this is hardly an obsession. The film is a work of art, for god's sake! What many seek on splattered canvas lining the walls of city art galleries, I can appreciate on the television screen.

In one scene, Miss Dalloway is introduced to Sir Russell, a New Zealand gentleman whom she befriends. Sir Russell is tall and handsome and speaks with an upper class accent. He is an expert polo player, politician and businessman. Clearly it is the scriptwriter's intention for Sir Russell to act as Miss Dalloway's friend and confidante; for his role, although not peripheral, is predominantly supportive. Sir Russell accompanies Miss Dalloway to the Mediterranean coast when she requires a respite from another broken heart. He is constantly at hand to offer solace or a sympathetic ear.

I have my suspicions about Sir Russell, however. There's something not quite right about that accent. I ought to know. I dated a Kiwi girl for two weeks to study it in more detail. I can't imagine what Sir Russell could possibly be doing in London. Besides, if he's such a hotshot in the business world, how can he afford to spend several weeks on the Mediterranean coast on a whim with Miss Dalloway? I may be naive but I cannot believe that this is the way to run a successful business!

At first, like everyone else in the movie theatre, I was pleased that Miss Dalloway had such a trusted friend on whom she could rely. Over time, however, as I studied the film again and again, I could pick out certain tremors in his accent, a quaver in his voice and four letter words in his body language. I can see through his deceit. I can tell he lusts after Miss Dalloway.

My girlfriend still believes I am obsessed. Just because I called her Julia the last time we made love.

I must confess it was really my fault. I don't know what I was thinking. The room was dark. Headlights from passing cars on the nearby motorway flickered through the curtains. The fan was whirring above our heads. I looked down and I honestly saw her.

GIRLFRIEND: My darling! Ooh! My darling!
MYSELF: Julia Dalloway!

Even as I said it I gasped. And exploded.

My girlfriend just can't forgive that mistake. Women are strange that way. Like elephants. They just can't forget.

To be fair, I must admit I harbour some passion for this movie. But surely passion is a good thing. *The Hideaway* is, after all, an hour and a half of cinematic perfection. I have often asked myself why it fascinates me so. How does it enrich me, nourish me so heartily when everything else tastes like bottled water?

Where does the magic come from? Is it the skill of Nathalie Hartman, who plays Miss Dalloway? Is it the spiritual direction of Scott McMahon? Is it, indeed, the subconscious expression of soul through the pen of Milson Bloom, the scriptwriter? I have tried to break the movie down into its individual facets in an effort to evaluate it but have come to the conclusion that its true success springs from the sum of its parts. Individually, the work of the actors, the writer, the cinematographer, the director and so on are delightful. Together, they form a masterpiece. That is all there is to say.

Several weeks ago my girlfriend left me; she said she'd finally had enough. She shouted and made a scene, clearly lacking the dignity that Miss Dalloway would have shown in such circumstances. And so ungracious! That very morning I'd bought her a business suit identical to one worn by Miss Dalloway. It was a stylish number with classical lines. Very becoming.

I felt that my girlfriend could use some assistance with style.

She kept shouting, "What is it with this bloody movie?" And yet, although I've patiently explained it to her several times, she just doesn't seem to get it. That is why such repetitious interrogation was so disappointing. Why can she not see that this movie is the epitome of soul-wrenching art? It is the hue of Polynesian flowers in a Gauguin painting. It is the first ray of sunshine after several weeks of rain. It is warm cocoa by the fire on a winter's night.

"It's fucking crap!" said my girlfriend. "It was a box-office failure! It won a Golden Turkey award, for god's sake!"

I don't miss my girlfriend. Although I do miss having someone else to talk to. Especially since I lost my job. I know it might sound a little silly but I did find it interfered with my work cataloguing the complete works and published critiques of *The Hideaway*. One day I hope to publish on the internet.

Last night I rang up every Miss Dalloway in the phone book. You'd be surprised by how many there are. After five answerphones, three wrong numbers, two changes of address, six severed connections and ten rude responses I realised that I was being ridiculous. The message had come from Sir Russell in London. That meant that Miss Dalloway wasn't **in** London but in another city.

Tomorrow I'll search the Birmingham telephone books. Although I'm sure that a woman of such breeding wouldn't be seen near the place, I can't afford to take any chances. My search must be precise. Elegant. Exact. Like the charming Miss Dalloway herself.

But now it's time to watch it again. I will continue my search tomorrow. Although the radio weatherman says that it'll rain, I remain optimistic. Somehow, I know it will be a lovely day.

ME: Yes a lovely day.

The title music swells.

FADE OUT
ROLL CREDITS

Morris dancing

The following papers have been donated to the National Archives by the Kaiwakawaka family of Westminster. All documents have been translated, as far as possible, into English.

Personal letter from Hemi Kaiwakawaka to the Whare o Te Io Confederation (1837)

Greetings three times, brothers

Seven long months have now passed since my arrival on the shores of New Aotearoa. The inhabitants of this land, the Britons, are a simple, superstitious people who enjoy nothing more than drinking fermented hops and arguing with their neighbours. With respect to diet, the southern inhabitants have a peculiar affection for tuber vegetables fried in natural oils. Those to the north are said to devour the entrails of sheep with great relish.

Many of the natives show great enthusiasm for kicking the bladder of a dead cow around a large field.

Despite my efforts to spread the joyful tidings of to matou Matua i te rangi [God] to the peoples of these isles, the existing peace has been significantly eroded by the recent introduction of the patu by unscrupulous Maori traders. Since the advent of this new technology, many of the southern peoples have used the military advantage conferred to invade the lands of their northern cousins. We have all been horrified by the unparalleled ferocity demonstrated as they occupy their neighbours' lands and make slaves of (or eat) their inhabitants.

Truly the Britons are a barbaric people!

Here in the safety of our little Westminster mission we are safe from the tribulations of the indigenes and have little real cause for concern. I do, however, question my suitability for a life as missionary at times. Thus far my 'conversions' have been more theoretical than practical in nature and some of the Britons appear frustratingly dense. Last week, during the christening of a local chieftain, I struck the ground with my taiaha in the customary flourish of celebration only to discover, later, that I'd actually stabbed him in the foot. When I questioned why he'd made no exclamation of display of outrage he said that he'd thought it was all part of the ceremony.

Io give me strength!

I confess that were it not for my successful work in the conversion of native Briton maidens I would surely consider returning to Aotearoa. Ah those exotic, white-skinned damsels! Brothers, pray for me.

Naku noa, na

Hemi Kaiwakawaka
Mihinare o Te Io
Westminster

PS. My seven children pass their greetings to their whanau in Aotearoa!

Personal letter from Hemi Kaiwakawaka to the Whare o Te Io Confederation (1845)

Greetings three times, brothers

Brothers, I report glad tidings! As a consequence of the ongoing threat of colonisation by the warlike Australians, a treaty has been signed with the Briton inhabitants that will finally bring law and order to this restless land.

This Treaty of Westminster was signed here in Westminster by representatives of the local people and it is with humility that I report my own contribution to this great deed — translating the document into the local tongue (Cornish). Admittedly, there was a certain element of confusion at first but everybody seemed happy enough to sign when we handed out those harakeke blankets and paua trinkets the Britons like so much.

Copies of the treaty have been transported around the whole island and, needless to say, we've highlighted the fact that it forms the basis for a unique partnership between our cultures. To my surprise, some of the returned copies have shown an impressive amount of artistic creativity. Due to the general illiteracy of the Britons, most of the signatures consist of a variety of colourful marks, smears and diagrams — many of which bear a disturbing similarity to a set of male genitalia.

In general, the natives have since demonstrated great fervour for the treaty and the sole rejection has been from the peoples of the nearby western isle who refuse to sign anything originating from their eastern cousins. A proclamation, nevertheless, has since been issued outlining the extension of our dominion to the entirety of both islands.

Nobody's told them yet but I'm sure they'll come around!

Naku noa, na

Hemi Kaiwakawaka
Mihinare o Te Io
Westminster

Personal letter from Paora Kaiwakawaka to Te Whanau o Kaiwakawaka, Wainuiomata, Aotearoa (1853)

Greetings three times, cousins

As tuakana, it is my sad duty to inform you that my father, Hemi, has finally boarded the waka for that fateful voyage back to Hawaiki. It pleases me to recount that he died at peace in bed — albeit not his own!

Although we regret his passing deeply, my father's legendary stamina will always be an inspiration to me, and my twenty-two brothers and three sisters.

We thank you also for your gifts of puha, flax and wildlife from Aotearoa. These have flourished in this country since their introduction and I recall my father was particularly gladdened by the sight of such familiar icons from his native land.

Here in New Aotearoa, the colonies of the Aotearoan Confederation of Tribes continue to thrive, particularly since the granting of representative government to the new settler communities. The role of

Governor has recently been filled by my own teina, Nika Kaiwakawaka. Although some dissatisfaction has been expressed by the locals, for the most part the Britons continue to treat our presence with enthusiasm and are quick to adopt our customs. In Westminster, for example, the topknot is now considered *de-rigueur* amongst the local Briton males. The beauty of the facial moko is also being embraced to tantalisingly effect by many of the more fashionable Briton women. For this reason I particularly resent a recent instruction from our kaumatua to curtail my late night 'forest grove' activities. I am shortly to be married to the daughter of an established Maori colonist family and my whanau are keen to ensure untainted Kaiwakawaka bloodlines.

Oh, well! As my father used to say: 'A manu in the hand is worth two in the bush!'"

Naku noa, na

Paora Kaiwakawaka
Westminster
New Aotearoa

Dispatch by Nika Kaiwakawaka — Governor of New Aotearoa to the Aotearoan Confederation of Tribes (1865)

Greetings three times

I give thanks for your continuing military and financial support in our struggle against the rebellious Britons. As reported in my last dispatch, large segments of the native population no longer seem to appreciate the opportunities offered to them by the government of New Aotearoa. Indeed, many of the ungrateful wretches have taken to open rebellion — particularly since the introduction of the fermented hops tax. Of all the Britons, the Windsor peoples have been the most vigorous in their resistance, successfully accumulating large numbers of supporters from other regions under the Windsor flag and calling themselves 'The King Movement'.

Needless to say, we have dealt firmly with pockets of the rebels, particularly along the western coast where large segments of land have been confiscated and offered to new Maori settlers. Some of the rascals have who have been removed from their lands have had the nerve to protest their innocence, claiming no knowledge of the events that had taken place and proclaiming vigorously to anyone who will listen that they are not Briton but Welsh.

(Whatever! They all look the same to me!)

To discourage Briton demands for a national constitution, I have allowed the temporary establishment of four Briton seats on the National Council of Chiefs. This is, of course, a temporary measure as I do not think it wise to allow semi-barbarous natives to frame a constitution for themselves. Despite this display of benevolence on my part, however, many Britons continue to complain of ongoing breaches to the treaty. Others continue to argue that the Briton seats give insufficient representation, given their numbers in the national population.

God, these bloody Britons whinge a lot!

Naku noa, na

Nika Kaiwakawaka
Governor
New Aotearoa

Letter from Pere Kaiwakawaka to Premier Chieftain of the New Aotearoa Government (1900)

Greetings three times

E hoa

I write to you today to express my great concern at the worsening condition of the noble Briton savage. Since the establishment of the colonies, the native population has continued to dwindle and now hovers on the brink of extinction. Much of this decline in population can be attributed to reproductive diseases introduced by the initial colonists (some blackguards attribute this directly to the activities of my beloved grandfather, Hemi!)

The Britons have also been affected drastically by the theft of their

Leannán Sidhe

lands and the destruction wrought by the introduction of wildlife from Aotearoa. Admittedly, even in retrospect, my father and his friends could not possibly have anticipated the impact these 'little reminders of the homeland' would have on native wildlife. Who could possibly have imagined that creatures such as the kakapo — so benignly inept in the wilds of Aotearoa — would adapt so ferociously to their new environment. In New Aotearoa, these feathered little terrorists revealed a hitherto unrecognised cunning and capacity for violence and are now known gang up in large numbers to attack defenceless stoats and weasels. The kiwi, too, has evolved dramatically in this country. According to rumours from the north, many of these avian fiends have somehow acquired the capacity for flight and developed the rather disturbing habit of 'buzzing' nesting swans.

Although I'd be the first to admit that the Britons can complain over-zealously on occasion, perhaps they have a point when it comes to the injurious impact of the Briton Land Act on their culture and society. The Britons are still losing large tracts of land as their individualised titles are absorbed into the tribal affiliations of the colonists. Those who remain in individual holdings lack the support of whanau and struggle to compete against the larger groupings. Is this, they ask, what it means to be a partner to the Aotearoa Confederation of Tribes? The theft of our land, the desecration of our culture, the loss of our traditional way of life?

If the boot was on the other waewae, could we honestly believe the Britons capable of treating us so badly? I don't think so!

Naku noa, na

Pere Kaiwakawaka
Westminster
New Aotearoa

Personal letter from Tane Kaiwakawaka to Pere Kaiwakawaka (1945)

Greetings, Father

I'm delighted to tell you that my wife and I have spent a very enjoyable honeymoon here on the Salisbury Plains. The weather has been excellent and we have taken the opportunity to partake in many of the local attractions. Oddly enough the most interesting of these was a three-day cultural experience package offered by one of the local native tourist companies. For the most part, this introduction to the renaissance of Briton culture consisted of frolicking naked amongst the heavenly edifices of a large stone circle and feasting on a diet of bacon butties (somewhat explaining the Briton predisposition to diabetes) and copious quantities of fermented hops. Although initially indisposed to what I've always considered a bunch of cultural and spiritual mumbo jumbo, over time and copious quantities of fermented hops, my cynicism began to soften. In fact, by the second day, I was experiencing spiritual visions of my own!

To be honest, I don't really remember much of what went on over large segments of my time there but I do remember the lightness of those milk-coated maidens as they danced between their sacred stones. At the time, however, I recall thinking how spiritually jaded us Maori have become in comparison to the Britons. The overall experience has left both my wife and I with a new-found respect for these noble and mystic people.

Honestly father, I recognise the fact that I may be something of a radical but as one comes to comprehend the Briton spirit, one actually starts to experience a certain degree of sympathy for some of their more violent protests. Perhaps it wasn't such a great idea, for example, to bulldoze Stonehenge to make way for new roads under the Public Works Act. I feel the recent resurgence of morris dancing is typical of the cultural backlash manifesting itself in our times. Although it cannot be denied that there is something majestic about the native Briton in those symbolic white costumes, the clash of the batons, the dynamic twirl of hankies and the thrilling jingle of bells, perhaps this is a prelude to some deeper ethnic awareness, the initiation of a cultural revolution that we can no longer ignore.

Naku noa, na

Tane Kaiwakawaka
Salisbury
New Aotearoa

Letter to the Office of Rangi Kaiwakawaka, tribal representative for Westminster (1991)

Greetings just once — I'm in a hurry!

I wish to express my disgust at the disgraceful behaviour of Briton activists at this year's Westminster Day celebrations. Citizens were not only exposed to an insulting demonstration of separatist dogma but also to an unprovoked and violent display of morris dancing. Can nothing prevent these British activists from their annual desecration of our nation's national day!

I'm tired of the continuing reference to the Treaty of Westminster. The treaty is not some magical, mystical, document. It certainly isn't any kind of rational blueprint for building a modern, prosperous, New Aotearoa. Bah! Throw it in the bin, I say!

Let's be pragmatic for once! The treaty did not create a partnership but a launching pad for the creation of one sovereign nation (that just so happened to be ours). Why can't those bloody Britons get used to the fact that we're all one people now? We are all New Aotearoans and if they don't want to be like us then they can just go back to sitting around campfires eating each other!

A. Nonymous
Bath
New Aotearoa

Diary extract of Rangi Kaiwakawaka, tribal representative for Westminster in the National Council of Chiefs and Minister of Briton Affairs (1995)

Dear Diary

Another brain-numbing encounter with Ben Drashist of the Westminster Action Committee this afternoon! Needless to say, it didn't take long before he was off on the usual tirade of complaints about treaty breaches, socio-economic disparities between Britons and Maori and so on. Fortunately, after years of select committee meetings I've developed the useful skill of sleeping with my eyes open. Much to my surprise, however, he was still going when I woke up almost twenty minutes later.

"What do you want me to do about it?' I growled. "I'm merely a simple politician.'

"Honour the bloody treaty!' he demanded. "Britons want to have a say in the governing of their own country. They don't want to be dictated to by a government that ridicules their culture and changes laws on a whim whenever it wants to further its own dominance.'

"Well, the Government does hold sovereignty," I pointed out.

"The Government assumed sovereignty. The Britons certainly never surrendered it!'

And off he went on another rant!

Unfortunately, 'organic intellectuals' like Mr Drashist do not appear to understand that possession is nine points of the law (note to self: draw up legislation to make it ten). Besides, the reallocation of national decision making powers is hardly a position that'll ever be supported by politicians, particularly when only a minority of the bloody population want it.

Although in general the Briton propensity for committees and infighting restricts the overall ability of individuals like Mr Drashist to mount any meaningful form of lobby group, I must admit that the recent organisation of a 'great march' to denounce government acquisition of the foreshore and our refusal to fly the Union Jack over London Bridge has taken us all a bit by surprise. At the end of our meeting, Mr Drashist had the gall to invite me to participate. Fortunately, I had the excuse of a prior engagement with a prize-winning sheep which for some reason, he found terribly amusing.

Bloody Britons! They were just lucky the Australian aboriginals didn't colonise them! They'd have sorted them out!

National Radio transcript of Rangi Kaiwakawaka - 'Nations Party' Address [Westminister Day — 2004]

[Transcript begins]

In these sad times, it is distressing to see the increasing impact of race-based policies on our society. When will these Britons understand!

None of us were around at the time of the New Aotearoa wars. None of us had anything to do with the confiscations — apart from having families that benefited. Honestly! There is a limit to how much any generation can apologise for the sins of its great-grandparents.

The truth is that those radicals who claim sovereignty never properly passed from Britons into the hands of the Aotearoa Confederation of Tribes, and thus ultimately into the hands of all New Aotearoans, are living in a fantasy world. They forget that today the majority of Briton children grow up with a non-Briton parent. Many people feel it is somehow impolite to mention these facts but I intend to do so anyway. Britons should no longer be permitted the luxury of considering themselves 'Briton', a separatist and divisive element of our great country. Under a 'Nations' Government, I can assure you we will rehabilitate these indigenes, heal them and absorb them into our society so that they can be like the rest of mainstream, so that they can — in effect — be like me!

Certainly, the indigenous culture of New Aotearoa will always hold a special place in our country, and will be cherished for that reason. A Nations Government will therefore continue to fund — to a limited degree — Cornish language classes, cricket and dead cow bladder sporting events — not because we have been conned into believing that that is somehow a special right enjoyed by Britons under the Treaty, but rather because ethnic celebrations are good for the tourist dollar and offer a degree of local colour during national celebrations.

Now, can I honestly be any fairer than that!

[Wet squelching thump]

Ouch! Bloody hell that hurt!
Who threw that bloody clod of earth!

[Transcripts Ends]